등신불

아시아에서는 《바이링궐 에디션 한국 대표 소설》을 기획하여 한국의 우수한 문학을 주제별로 엄선해 국내외 독자들에게 소개합니다. 이 기획은 국내외 우수한 번역가들이 참여하여 원작의 품격을 최대한 살렸습니다. 문학을 통해 아시아의 정체성과 가치를 살피는 데 주력해 온 아시아는 한국인의 삶을 넓고 깊게 이해하는 데 이 기획이 기여하기를 기대합니다.

Asia Publishers presents some of the very best modern Korean literature to readers worldwide through its new Korean literature series 〈Bilingual Edition Modern Korean Literature〉. We are proud and happy to offer it in the most authoritative translation by renowned translators of Korean literature. We hope that this series helps to build solid bridges between citizens of the world and Koreans through a rich in-depth understanding of Korea.

바이링궐 에디션 한국 대표 소설 107
Bi-lingual Edition Modern Korean Literature 107

Tŭngsin-bul

김동리
등신불

Kim Tong-ni

ASIA
PUBLISHERS

Contents

등신불

Tŭngsin-bul

등신불(等身佛)은 양자강(楊子江) 북쪽에 있는 정원사(淨願寺)의 금불각(金佛閣) 속에 안치되어 있는 불상(佛像)의 이름이다. 등신금불(等身金佛) 또는 그냥 금불이라고도 불렀다.

그러니까 나는 이 등신불, 또는 등신금불로 불리는 불상에 대해 보고 듣고 한 그대로를 여기다 적으려 하거니와, 그보다 먼저, 내가 어떻게 해서 그 정원사라는 먼 이역의 고찰(古刹)을 찾게 되었는지 그것부터 이야기해야겠다.

Tŭngsin-bul is the name of the Buddha enshrined in Kŭmbul-gak (Shrine of the Golden Buddha) at Chŏngwŏn-sa, a temple to the north of the Yangtze River. This statue of Buddha is also called Tŭngsin kŭmbul or just Kŭmbul (the Golden Buddha).

What I intend to do here is to write down what I have seen and heard of this Tŭngsin-bul or Tŭngsin kŭmbul. But first, I would like to tell my readers how it was that I had happened to pay a visit to this temple Chŏngwŏn-sa which is so far away, and in such a secluded place in a foreign land.

I was twenty-two years old and was attending Taejŏng University in Japan when I was drafted as a

내가 일본의 대정대학 재학 중에, 학병(태평양전쟁)으로 끌려 나간 것은 일구사삼년(1943년) 이른 여름, 내 나이 스물세 살 나던 때였다.

내가 소속된 부대는 북경(北京)서 서주(徐州)를 거쳐 남경(南京)에 도착했었다. 그리하여 우리는 다른 부대가 당도할 때까지 거기서 머무르게 되었다. 처음엔 주둔(駐屯)이라기보다 대기(待機)에 속하는 편이었으나, 다음 부대의 도착이 예상보다 늦어지자, 나중은 교체 부대(交替部隊)가 당도할 때까지 주둔군(駐屯軍)의 임무를 맡게 되었다.

그때 우리는 확실한 정보는 아니지만 대체로 인도지나나 인도네시아 방면으로 가게 된다는 것을 어림으로 짐작하고 있었기 때문에, 하루라도 오래 남경에 머물면 머물수록 그만치 우리의 목숨이 더 연장되는 거와 같이 생각하고 있었다. 따라서 교체 부대가 하루라도 더 늦게 와주었으면 하고 마음속으로 은근히 빌고 있는 편이기도 했다.

실상은 그냥 빌고 있는 심정만도 아니었다. 더 나아가서 이 기회에 기어이 나는 나의 목숨을 건져내어야 한다고 결심을 했다. 나는 이런 기회를 위하여 미리 약간

student soldier to fight in the Japanese Army. It was in the early summer of 1943.

The detachment to which I was allocated went to Peking and from there to Nanking by way of Soochow. We were supposed to stay in that city until another detachment should arrive. However, as our period of waiting prolonged, our status in the city became more like that of a garrison than that of troops in temporary stay. In the meantime, we were performing general duties of a garrison, too.

Although vaguely, we knew that when we should be moved out of Nanking, we would be sent to either Indochina or Indonesia.

Therefore, few of us regretted the delay in the arrival of another detachment to relieve us from our garrison duties. Rather, most of us harbored a wish that we be detained in Nanking as long as possible because it meant keeping ourselves alive that much longer.

In my case, it was not just wishful thinking. On the contrary, I was determined that I would try whatever method available to save myself before the detachment should be transferred out of Nanking. In fact, I had done some "research work" in order to materialize this plan in case a proper op-

의 준비(조사)까지 해두었던 것이다. 그것은 중국의 불교 학자(佛教學者)로서 일본에 와 유학을 하고 돌아간—특히 대정대학 출신으로—사람들의 명단을 조사해 둔 일이었다. 나는 비장(秘藏)한 작은 쪽지에서 '남경 진기수(陳奇修)'란 이름을 발견했을 때 야릇한 흥분으로 가슴이 후들거리며 머릿속까지 휑해지는 듯했다.

그러나 낯선 이역의 도시에서, 더구나 나 같은 일본군에 소속된 한국 출신 학병의 몸으로서, 그를 찾고 못 찾고 하는 일이 곧 내가 죽고 사는 판가름이라고 생각하지 않았던들, 또 내가 평소에 나의 책상머리에 언제나 걸어두고 바라보던 관세음보살님의 미소로써 나를 굽어보고 있는 것이라고 믿어지지 않았던들, 그때의 그러한 용기와 지혜를 내 속에서 나는 자아내지 못했을는지 모른다.

나는 우리 부대가 앞으로 사흘 이내에 남경을 떠난다고 하는—그것도 확실한 정보가 아니고 누구의 입에선가 새어나온 말이지만—조마조마한 고비에 정심원(靜心院)—남경에 있는 중국인 불교 포교당—에 있는 포교사(布教師)를 통하여 진기수 씨가 남경 교외의 서공암(捿空庵)이라는 작은 암자에 독거(獨居)하고 있다는 것을

portunity should present itself. My research work consisted of making a list of Chinese Buddhist scholars who had studied in Japan (especially those who studied at Taejŏng University). When I found the name "Chin Ki-su" given as a resident of Nanking on a sheet of secret documents, I was so excited that I nearly felt faint.

However, it was not easy for a Korean soldier belonging to the Japanese Army to look up a man in a foreign city. If finding him had not been a matter of life and death for me, and if the image of the Merciful Goddess had not smiled down at me constantly from her place on the wall, I doubt that I should have had the courage and wit to really find the man and make him help me with my plans.

At a crucial time when there was information, or rather, a rumor spreading about our detachment leaving Nanking within three days, I came to learn from a monk who belonged to a Buddhist missionary corps in Nanking called Chŏngsim-wŏn that Mr. Chin Ki-su was residing at the moment at a hermitage Sŏgong-am in complete solitude.

It was when dusk started to descend on the city of Nanking that I paid a visit to Mr. Chin Ki-su at his little temple or hermitage. I folded my hands in *hap-*

알게 되었다.

그날 내가 서공암에서 진기수 씨를 찾게 된 것은 땅거미가 질 무렵이었다. 나는 그를 보자 합장을 올리며 무수히 머리를 수그림으로써 나의 절박한 사정과 그에 대한 경의를 먼저 표한 뒤, 솔직하게 나의 처지와 용건을 털어놓았다.

그러나 평생 처음 보는 타국 청년—그것도 적국의 군복을 입은—에게 그러한 위험한 협조를 쉽사리 약속해 줄 사람은 없었다. 그의 두 눈이 약간 찡그려지며 입에서는 곧 거절의 선고가 내릴 듯한 순간, 나는 미리 준비하고 갔던 흰 종이를 끄집어내어 내 앞에 폈다. 그러고는 바른편 손 식지 끝을 스스로 물어서 살을 떼어낸 다음 그 피로써 다음과 같이 썼다.

願免殺生 歸依佛恩 (원컨대 살생을 면하게 하옵시며 부처님의 은혜 속에 귀의코자 하나이다).

나는 이 여덟 글자의 혈서를 두 손으로 받들어 그의 앞에 올린 뒤 다시 합장을 했다.

이것을 본 진기수 씨는 분명히 얼굴빛이 달라졌다. 그

jang (Buddhist practice of folding hands in greeting or pray) as soon as I saw him and kotowed many times so that he might understand it was out of sincere respect for his holy devotion to religion and the urgency of the situation in which I found myself that I dared to appear before him like that. After this preliminary ceremony, I told him my circumstances as well as I could.

But, from his point of view, I was an utter stranger, a soldier belonging to the enemy camp at that. I saw that his eyebrows were knitted in an expression of displeasure. But just as words of refusal to my entreaty were about to fall from his mouth (or at least I thought they were), I took out the white sheet of paper I had prepared beforehand and, biting a morsel of flesh off my index finger, wrote with the blood that flowed out of the wound: *Wŏnmyŏnsalsaeng Kwiŭibulŭn* (願免殺生 歸依佛恩) which meant that I wanted to be exempted from the offence of life-taking and to reside in the merciful world of Buddha forever.

I offered these eight characters written in blood to him and again folded my hands in *hapjang*.

I seemed to see a change in the expression on Mr. Chin Ki-su's face. The expression I saw now was

것은 반드시 기쁜 빛이라 할 수는 없었으나 조금 전의 그 거절의 선고만은 가셔진 듯한 얼굴이었다.

잠깐 동안 침묵이 흐른 뒤, 진기수 씨는 나직한 목소리로 입을 열었다.

"나를 따라오게."

나는 곧 자리에서 일어나 그의 뒤를 따라갔다.

깊숙한 골방이었다.

진기수 씨는 나를 그 컴컴한 골방 속에 들여보내고 자기는 문을 닫고 도로 나가버렸다. 조금 뒤 그는 법의(法衣: 중국 승려복) 한 벌을 가져와 방 안으로 디밀며,

"이걸로 갈아입게."

하고 또 다시 문을 닫고 나갔다.

나는 한숨이 터져 나왔다. 이제야 사는가 보다 하는 생각이 나의 가슴속을 후끈하게 적셔주는 듯했다.

내가 옷을 갈아입고 났을 때, 이번에는 또 간소한 저녁상이 디밀어졌다.

나는 말없이 디밀어진 저녁상을 또한 그렇게 말없이 받아서 지체 없이 다 먹어 치웠다.

내가 빈 그릇을 문 밖으로 내어놓자 밖에서 기다리고나 있었던 듯 이내 진기수 씨가 어떤 늙은 중 하나를 데

not exactly that of delight or contentment but at least it was devoid of the firm air of refusal it had before.

After a brief silence, Mr. Chin Ki-su said:

"Follow me."

I got up at once and hurried after him.

It was a small room in the innermost part of the building that Mr. Chin Ki-su took me to. He left me in this room and walked away after closing the door. After a while however, he came back with a suit of monk's clothes and said:

"Change into these."

After these words, he left the room again closing the door after him.

I breathed a long sigh of relief. For the first time, I felt that now I would be able to live.

When I changed into the monk's clothes, I was given a simple supper on a tray which was pushed into the room. I took the tray without a word and ate up everything quickly.

As soon as I pushed the tray back into the hall outside the room, Mr. Chin Ki-su came in with an old monk as if they had been waiting right outside my room while I ate.

"Go with him," he said. "I gave my letter of intro-

리고 들어왔다.

"이분을 따라가게. 소개장은 이분에게 맡겼어. 큰절[本刹]의 내 법사 스님한테 가는……."

"……."

나는 무조건 네, 네, 하며 곧장 머리를 끄덕일 뿐이었다. 나를 살려주려는 사람에게 무조건 나를 맡길 수밖에 없었던 것이다.

"길은 일본 병정들이 알지도 못하는 산속 지름길이야. 한 백 리 남짓 되지만, 오늘이 스무하루니까 밤중 되면 달빛도 좀 있을 게구…… 그럼…… 불연(佛緣) 깊기를…… 나무관세음보살."

그는 나를 향해 합장을 하며 머리를 수그렸다.

"……"

나는 목이 콱 메여옴을 깨달았다. 눈물이 핑 돈 채, 나도 그를 향해 잠자코 합장을 올렸다.

어둡고 험한 산길을 경암(鏡岩)—나를 데리고 가는 늙은 중—은 거침없이 걸었다. 아무리 발에 익은 길이라 하지만 군데군데 나뭇가지가 걸리고 바닥이 패고 돌이 솟고 게다가 굽이굽이 간수(澗水)[1]가 가로지른 초망(草

duction to him. The letter is addressed to the father monk of the main temple."

I did not venture to say anything but merely bowed my head again and again in complete obeisance. What else could I do when he was the only one in the whole wide world who could save my life? I entrusted myself to him entirely.

"The road which you will take is not known to the Japanese soldiers. It's a mountain path. It's about one hundred *ri* (40 kilometers) from here. Today is the twenty-first, however, and there will be some moonlight later on, I believe. Well, then. I pray that Buddha's protection stay with you. *Namugwanseŭmbosal* (a Buddhist invocation)."

Mr. Chin Ki-su folded his hands and bowed to me. I could not find a word to say to him. My throat choked and tears welled up in my eyes. In this state, I folded my hands and bowed back to him.

Kyŏngam—the old monk who led me—walked fast inspite of the darkness and un-evenness of the road. No doubt he was accustomned to this mountain route. Still, apart from the darkness, there were stray fallen branches to catch one's feet, and holes where the earth sunk, edges of rocks pushing out of the ground where their main bodies were bur-

葬)[2] 속의 지름길을 칠흑 같은 어둠 속에서 어쩌면 그렇게도 잘 뚫고 나가는지 그저 신기하기만 했다. 내가 믿는 것은 젊음 하나뿐이련만, 그는 이십 리나 삼십 리를 걸어도 힘에 부치어 쉬자고 할 기색은 보이지 않았다.

나는 쉴 새 없이 손으로 이마의 땀을 씻어가며, 그의 뒤를 따랐으나 한참씩 가다 보면 어느덧 그를 어둠 속에 잃어버리곤 했다. 나는 몇 번이나 나뭇가지에 얼굴이 긁히고, 돌에 채어 무릎을 깨고 하며, "대사……" "대사……" 그를 불러야만 했다. 그럴 때마다 경암은 혼잣말로 낮게 중얼거리며 나를 기다려주는 것이나, 내가 가까이 가면 또 아무 말도 없이 그냥 획 돌아서서 걸음을 옮겨놓기 시작하는 것이다.

밤중도 훨씬 넘어 조각달이 수풀 사이로 비쳐들면서부터 나는 비로소 생기를 얻기 시작했다. 이제부터는 경암이 제아무리 앞에서 달린다 하더라도 두 번 다시 그를 놓치지는 않으리라 맘속으로 다짐했다.

이렇게 정세가 바뀌었음을 그도 느끼는지 내가 그의 곁으로 다가서자 그는 나를 흘낏 돌아다보더니, 한쪽 팔을 들어 먼 데를 가리키며 반원을 그어 보이고는 이백 리라고 했다. 이렇게 지름길을 가지 않고 좋은 길로

ied. And this was not all. There were even occasional streams crossing the path which Was nearly hidden by the thick growth of grass. But all these impediments were nothing to the old monk, apparently. He walked just as easily as if he were walking on an open smooth road. The only advantage I had over him was that I was much younger than he was.

I soon realized, however, that he was not going to allow me even this one upper hand. Because after walking as much as thirty *ri*, he was still not tired and did not suggest a break.

I struggled after him with all my might, constantly wiping away the sweat that broke out on my forehead. Still, more often than not, I lost him in the darkness and was driven to a panic. Moreover, the branches of trees scratched at my face and I kept falling over the protruding rocks and hurt myself which put a further distance between me and the old monk. Many times, I had to call out to him: "Master!" "Master!" Kyŏngam would stop when he was called and mumbling something in his mouth would wait for me to catch up. But the minute I appeared within sight, he would turn about and walk on swiftly.

It was long after midnight when the crescent

돌아가면 이백 리 길이라는 뜻인 듯했다.

나는 한마디 얻어들은 중국말로 "셰 셰" 하고 장단을 맞추며 고개를 끄덕여 보이곤 했다.

우리가 정원사 산문 앞에 닿았을 때는 이튿날 늦은 아침녘이었다. 경암은 푸른 수풀 속에 거뭇거뭇 보이는 높은 기와집들을 손가락질로 가리키며 자랑스런 얼굴로 무어라고 중얼거렸다. 나는 또 고개를 끄덕이며 "하오! 하오!"를 되풀이했다.

산문을 지나 정문을 들어서니 산무더기 같은 큰 다락이 정면에 버티고 섰다. 현판을 쳐다보니 태허루(太虛樓)라 씌어 있었다.

태허루 곁을 돌아 안마당 어귀에 들어서니 정면 한가운데 높직이 앉아 있는 가장 웅장한 건물이 법당이라고 짐작이 가나 그 양옆으로 첩첩이 가로세로 혹은 길쭉하게 눕고, 혹은 높다랗게 서고 혹은 둥실하게 앉은 무수한 집들이 모두 무슨 이름에 어떠한 구실을 하는 것들인지 첫눈엔 그저 황홀하고 얼떨떨할 뿐이었다.

경암은 나를 데리고, 그 첩첩이 둘러앉은 집들 사이를 한참 돌더니 청정실(淸淨室)이란 조그만 현판이 붙은 조용한 집 앞에 와서 기척을 했다. 방문이 열리더니 한 스

moon appeared in the sky and began to light up our road with its dim illumination. I was immensely relieved by this and from this time on could walk after Kyŏngam with more ease and speed. I said to myself that from this point, I will never again lose sight of Kyŏngam no matter how fast he walked.

Maybe the old monk sensed the change in our situation. When I came up to him, he turned a rather sociable face to me, and raising his one arm and drawing a semicircle with it toward a distant sky, said: "Two hundred *ri*." He seemed to mean that if we had taken the smooth good road to the temple instead of this steep short-cut, the journey would have amounted to two hundred *ri*.

I repeated "yes," "yes," (about the only Chinese I knew) and nodded my head busily.

It was late next morning that we arrived in front of the outer gate of Chŏngwŏn-sa. Kyŏngam pointed to the tile-roofed buildings that showed between the trees and said something I could not understand. His face beamed with pride as he pointed out the dark-tiled buildings to me. I nodded my head again heartily and said: "Good. Good."

We entered through the outer gate and then the main gate. Suddenly, I was faced with a tremen-

무 살이나 될락 말락 한 젊은 중이 얼굴을 내밀며 알은 체를 한다. 둘이서 (젊은이는 방문 앞에 서고 경암은 뜰 아래 선 채) 한참 동안 말을 주고받고 한 끝에 경암이 나를 데리고 집 안으로 들어갔다.

방 안에는 머리가 하얗게 세고 키가 성큼하게 커 뵈는 노승이 미소 띤 얼굴로 경암과 나를 맞아주었다. 나는 말이 통하지 않으므로 노승 앞에 발을 모으고 서서 정중히 합장을 올렸다. 어저께 진기수 씨 앞에서 연거푸 머리를 수그리던 것과는 달리, 이번에는 한 번만 정중하게 머리를 수그려 절을 했던 것이다.

노승은 미소 띤 얼굴로 고개를 끄덕이며 나에게 앉을 자리를 가리킨 뒤 경암이 내드린 진기수 씨의 편지를 펴보았다.

"불은(佛恩)이로다."

편지를 읽고 난 노승은 이렇게 말했다. (그것도 그때는 알아듣지 못했지만 나중 가서 알고 보니 그랬다. 그리고 이것도 나중에야 알게 된 일이지만, 이 노승이 두어 해 전까지 이 절의 주지[住持]를 지낸 원혜대사[圓慧大師]로, 진기수 씨가 말한 자기의 법사[法師] 스님이란 곧 이분이었던 것이다.)

그날 저녁때 나는 원혜대사의 주선으로 그가 거처하

dously huge garret that loomed in the front. The signboard said T'aehŏru.

We went round T'aehŏru and went into the inner court. Straight opposite the entrance of the inner court was a big building that was raised up high over the stone terrace. I guessed that this must be the hall of worship. But I had no way of telling what were the numerous other buildings that lay side-ways, lenght-wise, low, and high to both sides of the central building. I was just overwhelmed by their majesty and a little confused.

Kyŏngam led me through many an alley between these buildings and finally stopped in front of a little house with a signboard: that said Ch'ŏngjŏngsil. As he made the coughing signal, the door in the front of the house opened and a young monk about the age of twenty pushed his head out. He made a greeting sign to Kyŏngam. The two of them, the young monk standing at the doorway and the old monk standing outside the door, conversed for some time. Finally, Kyŏngam motioned me to follow him into the house.

A tall old man with completely white hair greeted us with a smile as we entered the room. Since I did not know any Chinese except the couple of words,

고 있는 청정실 바로 곁의 조그만 방 한 칸을 혼자서 쓸 수 있게 되었다.

나를 그 방으로 인도해 준 젊은이—원혜대사의 시봉(侍奉)—는,

"저와 이웃이죠."

희고 넓적한 이를 드러내 보이며 빙긋이 웃었다. 그리고 자기 이름을 청운(淸雲)이라 부른다고 했다.

나는 방 한 칸을 따로 쓰고 있었지만, 결코 방 안에 들어앉아 게으름을 피우지는 않았다. 나를 죽을 고비에서 건져준 진기수 씨—그의 법명(法名)은 혜운(慧雲)이었다—나 원혜대사의 은덕을 생각해서라도 나는 결코 남의 입질에 오르내릴 짓을 해서는 안 되리라고 결심했던 것이다.

나는 아침 일찍이 일어나 세수를 하고, 예불을 끝내면 청운과 함께 청정실 안팎과 앞뒤의 복도와 뜰을 먼지 티끌 하나 없이 쓸고 닦았다.

뿐만 아니라, 다른 스님들을 따라 산에 가 약초도 캐고 식량 준비도 거들었다. (이 절에서도 전쟁 관계로 식량이 딸렸으므로 산중의 스님들은 여름부터 식용이 될 만한 풀잎과 나

I contented myself with folding my hands and bowing to him very politely.

The white-haired monk was smiling and nodding his head. He then opened the letter from Mr. Chin Ki-su handed him by Kyŏngam who had in the meantime designated me a place to sit down.

"This is the blessing of Buddha," said the elder monk after reading the letter from Mr. Chin Ki-su. (I did not understand what he said at the time but found out the meaning of his words later on when my understanding of Chinese improved. Later, I also found out that this white-haired old monk was the very person Mr. Chin Ki-su had called "the father monk," and that his proper sacred name was Master Wŏnhye and that he had been the head monk of this temple until two years ago.)

That night, I slept in a small room next to Ch'ŏngjŏngsil where the old master resided. The young monk who led me to my new abode—he was a kind of secretary to the old master—said: "I am your neighbor," and grinned widely. He said he was called Ch'ŏngun (Clear Cloud).

Although I was thus alotted a separate room and a kind of independence along with it, I did not spend my time idling. I did not wish to betray the trust and goodness Mr.Chin Ki-su—(his sacred name

무뿌리 같은 것들을 캐러 산으로 가곤 했다.)

일을 마치고 돌아오면 손발을 깨끗이 씻고 내 방에 꿇어앉아 불경을 읽거나 그렇지 않으면 청운에게 중국어를 배웠다. (이것은 나의 열성에다 청운의 호의가 곁들어서 그런지 의외로 빨리 진척이 되어 사흘 만에 이미 간단한 말로—물론 몇 마디씩이지만—대화하는 흉내까지 낼 수 있게 되었다.)

아무리 방에 혼자 있을 때라도 취침 시간 이외엔 방 안에 번듯이 드러눕지 않도록 나 자신과 씨름을 했다. 그렇게 버릇을 들이지 않으려고 나는 몇 번이나 나 자신에게 다짐을 놓았는지 모른다. 졸음이 와서 정 견디기가 어려울 때는 밖으로 나와 어정대며 바람을 쐬곤 했다.

처음엔 이렇게 막연히 어정대며 바람을 쐬던 것이 얼마 가지 않아 나는 어정대지 않게 되었다. 으레 가는 곳이 정해지게 되었다. 그것이 저 금불각(金佛閣)이었던 것이다.

여기서도 물론 나는 법당 구경을 먼저 했다. 본존(本尊)을 모셔둔 곳이니만치 그 절의 풍도나 품격을 가장 대표적으로 보여주는 곳이라는 까닭으로서보다도 절 구경은 으레 법당이 중심이라는 종래의 습관 때문이라

was Hyeun) and Master Wŏnhye showed me. I made up my mind that I would not behave in such a way as would bring disgrace to either of them.

Consequently, I was up and around at the earliest possible hour, washing myself up, offering early morning prayers, and cleaning, along with Ch'ŏngun, the halls and courtyards surrounding Ch'ŏngjŏngsil.

I also followed after the monks when they went around in the mountains to collect herbs for medicine and food. (As everywhere else, food was getting scarce in this temple and so the monks went around the mountains to gather edible plants and roots.)

After work, I came back to my room with my hands and feet washed up and either read the Buddhist scriptures or learned Chinese from Ch'ŏngun. (This project was more successful than I had expected, and after only a few days' studying, I could exchange some simple words with my teacher although they were only very rudimentary in content.)

I tried not to lie down or rest in any sloppy way even if I was in my room by myself until it became time for me to sleep at night. I really put myself into this effort. When I felt so sleepy that I could not sit up straight, I went out of my room and walked about so as not to lie down before bedtime.

고 하는 편이 옳았는지 모른다. 그러나 내가 법당에서 얻은 감명은 우리나라의 큰절이나 일본의 그것에 견주어 그렇게 자별하다고 할 것이 없었다. 기둥이 더 굵대야 그저 그렇고, 불상이 더 크대야 놀랄 정도는 아니요, 그 밖에 채색이나 조각에 있어서도 한국이나 일본의 그것에 비하여 더 정교(精巧)한 편은 아닌 듯했다. 다만 정면 한가운데 높직이 모셔져 있는 세 위(位)의 불상(훌륭히 도금을 입힌)을 그대로 살아 있는 사람으로 간주하고 힘겨룸을 시켜본다면 한국이나 일본의 그것보다 더 놀라운 힘을 쓸 수 있지 않을까 하는 생각이었다. 그러니까 나로서는 어디까지나 '살아 있는 사람으로 간주하고 힘겨룸을 시켜본다면' 하는 가정에서 말한 것이지만, 그네의 눈으로써 보면 자기네의 부처님(불상)이 그만치 더 거룩하게만 보일는지 모를 일이었다. 더 쉽게 말하자면, 내가 위에서 말한 더 놀라운 힘이란 체력(體力)을 뜻하는 것이지만, 그들의 눈에는 그것이 어떤 거룩한 법력(法力)이나 도력(道力)으로 비칠는지도 모른다는 것이다.

그리고 내가 특히 이런 생각을 더하게 된 것은 금불각을 구경한 뒤였다. 금불각 속에 모셔져 있는 등신불

When I roamed out of my abode in this way, I did not at first know where to go. But I soon stopped roaming. Because I found a destination. It was a shrine called Kŭmbul-gak.

I looked at the hall of worship, first, I did not do this because I necessarily believed that being the place where the principal image is installed, it would best illustrate the general climate and standing of the shrine among Buddhist worshipping places. I think the reason why I looked at the hall of worship first was simply that it had become habitual with me (as probably with many other people) to start a tour of a Buddhist temple or shrine from the main hall of worship. My inspection of the hall, however, assured me that there was nothing very special about it compared with the main halls of the temples or shrines I had seen in Korea or Japan up to that time. It may be that it had thicker pillars, bigger images, but the differences, if there were any, were negligible. The painting and the sculpturing also were not any more sophisticated or artistic compared with the main halls of other worshipping places I had seen. If I were pressed to point out any mentionable characteristic of this place, I might say that the three gilt statues of Buddha in the front

(등신금불)을 보고 받은 깊은 감명이, 그 절의 모든 것을, 특히 법당에 모셔져 있는 세 위의 큰 불상을, 거룩하게 느끼게 하는 어떤 압력 같은 것이 되어 나타났다고나 할까.

물론 나는 청운이나 원혜대사로부터 금불각에 대하여 미리 들은 바는 없었지만 금불각이 앉은 자리라든가 그 집 구조로 보아서 약간 특이한 느낌이 그 안의 불상(등신불)을 구경하기 전에 이미 들지 않았던 것은 아니다. 그것은 무엇보다도 법당 뒤꼍에서 길 반가량 높이의 돌계단을 올라가서, 거기서부터 약 오륙십 미터 거리의 경사진 석대(石臺)가 구축되고, 그 석대가 곧 금불각에 이르는 길이 되어 있기 때문인지도 몰랐다. 더구나 그 석대가 꼭 같은 크기의 넓적넓적한 네모잽이 돌로 쌓아져 있는데 돌 위엔 보기 좋게 거뭇거뭇한 돌 옷이 입혀져 있었던 것이다. 말하자면 법당 뒤꼍의 동북쪽 언덕을 보기 좋은 돌로 평평하게 쌓아서 석대를 만들고 그 위에 금불각을 세워 놓은 것이다. 게다가 추녀와 현판을 모두 돌아가며 도금을 입히고 네 벽에 새긴 조상(彫像)과 그림에 도금을 많이 써서 그야말로 밖에서 보는 건물 그 자체부터 금빛이 현란했다.

looked as if they might come out the winners in a contest of strength with the other statues I had seen elsewhere. That is, the Buddhas in this shrine looked physically stronger than the Buddhas of other places. However, this was entirely my own subjective impression of the place. To those who worshiped here, what appeared to me as their superior physical strength must have looked like so much more saintliness. Maybe it was after I happened to take a look at the golden statue of Buddha of this shrine that I began to associate the three Buddhas in the main hall of worship with saintliness or spiritual power. Because the sight of the golden Buddha seemed gradually to throw a new light of holiness over everything I saw in the place including the three Buddhas.

I had not heard from either Ch'ŏngun or Master Wŏnhye about the Shrine of the Statue of the Golden Buddha. From the way the shrine was constructed and situated, however, I had had some idea of the peculiar circumstances in which I would find the Golden Buddha installed inside the shrine. One of these circumstances was that the shrine was built on top of about a fifty square meter stone terrace which was built in its turn on elevated terrain which

나는 본디 비단이나, 종이나, 나무나, 쇠붙이 따위에 올린 금물이나 금박 같은 것을 왠지 거북해하는 성미라 금불각에 입혀져 있는 금빛에도 그러한 경계심(警戒心)과 반감 같은 것을 품고 대했지만, 하여간 이렇게 석대를 쌓고 금칠을 하고 할 때는 그대들로서 무언가 아끼고 위하는 마음의 표시를 하느라고 한 짓임에 틀림없을 것이라고 보지 않을 수 없었다.

그러면서도 나는 그 아끼고 위하는 것이 보나마나 대단한 것은 아니리라고 혼자 속으로 미리 단정을 하고 있었다. 나의 과거 경험으로 본다면, 이런 것은 대개 어느 대왕(大王)이나 황제(皇帝)의 갸륵한 뜻으로 순금을 많이 넣어서 주조(鑄造)한 불상이라든지 또는 어느 천자가 어느 황후의 명복을 빌기 위해서 친히 불사를 일으킨 연유의 불상이라든지 하는 따위—대왕이나 황제의 권위를 보여주기 위한 금빛이 십상이었기 때문이었다.

나의 이러한 생각은 그들이 이 금불각의 권위를 높이기 위하여 좀처럼 문을 열어주지 않는 것을 보고 더욱 굳어졌다. 적어도 은화(銀貨) 다섯 냥 이상의 새전(賽錢)이 아니면 문을 여는 법이 없다는 것이다. 그렇지 않으

one had to reach from the road by a set of stone steps. The terrace was made up of square-shaped stones whose surface was covered with dark moss in a charming design. To put it more simply, they had covered the hill that stood at the back of the main hall with good looking square stone and built a shrine for the golden statue on top of it. They had painted the eaves of the shrine and the signboard all in gold and also used much gold in decorating the engravings and the pictures. Therefore, looking from the outside, the building itself shone in heavy gold.

I had not had much liking for the golden paint or plating that was used on silk, paper, wood or metal. Therefore, I felt some antipathy at first toward the golden ornamentation on Kŭmbul-gak also. It was undeniable, however, that to those who built it and those who worshipped there, the place had a very special meaning. So much elaborate decorating could not have been done without a very special feeling of adoration and maybe affection, as well, I thought.

In my mind, however, I decided that whatever it was that the people so much adored and valued and guarded in such a special manner inside the

면 어느 선남선녀의 큰 불공이 있을 때라야만 한다는 것이다. (그리고 이때—큰 불공이 있을—에도 본사 승려 이외에 금불각을 참례하는 자는 또 따로 새전을 내야 한다는 것이다.)

그렇다면 더구나 신도들의 새전을 긁어모으기 위한 술책으로 좁쌀만 한 언턱거리를 가지고 연극을 꾸미고 있는 것임이 틀림이 없으리라고 나는 아주 단정을 하고 도로 내 방으로 돌아왔다가 그때 마침 청운이 중국어를 가르쳐 주려고 왔기에,

"저 금불각이란 게 뭐지?"

아무것도 아닌 것처럼 물어보았다.

"왜요?"

청운이 빙긋이 웃으며 도로 물었다.

"구경 갔더니 문을 안 열어주던데……."

"지금 같이 가볼까요?"

"무어, 담에 보지."

"담에라도 그럴 거예요, 이왕 맘 난 김에 가보시구려."

청운이 은근히 권하는 빛이기도 해서 나는 그렇다면 하고 그를 따라 나갔다.

이번에는 청운이 숫제 금불각을 담당한 노승에게서 쇳대[3]를 빌려와서 손수 문을 열어주었다. 그리고 문 앞

shrine could not amount to anything much. Because my past experience had taught me that usually it was either the statues of Buddha on which some magnanimous royalty bestowed a substantial amount of gold or the Buddha which was built by some king in commemoration of his dead queen, a mere showy manifestation of power.

My conviction about the golden statue grew firmer as they refused to open the door of the shrine to me. I was told that unless one brought five silver pieces of offerings, the door would not be opened. Another occasion when the door opened was when there were prayers on behalf of some important personages. But even at these times, unless one was a monk belonging to Chŏngwŏn-sa, one had to offer money to be allowed to enter the shrine.

As I learned more about it, my conviction that Kŭmbul-gak was nothing more than a gimmick invented to draw money out of the pockets of the believers grew firmer and I was ready to believe nothing else.

When Ch'ŏngun came to my room to teach me Chinese, however, I asked him pretending nonchalance:

"What is Kŭmbul-gak, I mean that thing over there?"

에 선 채 그도 합장을 올렸다.

나는 그가 문을 여는 순간부터 미묘한 충격에 사로잡힌 채 그가 합장을 올릴 때도 그냥 멍하니 불상만 바라보고 서 있었다. 우선 내가 예상한 대로 좀 두텁게 도금을 입힌 불상임에는 틀림이 없었다. 그러나 그것은 전혀 내가 미리 예상했던 그러한 어떤 불상이 아니었다. 머리 위에 향로를 이고, 두 손을 합장한, 고개와 등이 앞으로 좀 수그러진, 입도 조금 헤벌어진, 그것은 불상이라고 할 수도 없는, 형편없이 초라한, 그러면서도 무언지 보는 사람의 가슴을 쥐어짜는 듯한, 사무치게 애절한 느낌을 주는 등신대(等身大)의 결가부좌상(結跏趺坐像)이었다. 그렇게 정연하고 단아하게 석대를 쌓고 추녀와 현판에 금물을 입힌 금불각 속에 안치되어 있음직한, 아름답고 거룩하고 존엄성 있는 그러한 불상과는 하늘과 땅 사이라고나 할까, 너무도 거리가 먼, 어이가 없는, 허리도 제대로 펴고 앉지 못한, 머리 위에 조그만 향로를 얹은 채 우는 듯한, 웃는 듯한, 찡그린 듯한, 오뇌와 비원(悲願)이 서린 듯한, 그러면서 무어라고 형언할 수 없는 슬픔이랄까 아픔 같은 것이 보는 사람의 가슴을 콱 움켜잡는 듯한, 일찍 본 적도 상상한 적도 없는

"Why do you ask?"

Ch'ŏngun asked back with a meaningful smile.

"They would not open the door for me to take a look."

"Shall we go back now and try again?"

"I don't think that's necessary. There will be another time."

"It will be the same even then. Come on. Let's go and see what happens while your mind is bent that way."

As if to oblige Ch'ŏngun, I got up and followed him.

Ch'ŏngun went and borrowed the key from the old monk who was in charge of the shrine. After he opened the door, he stood deferentially with folded hands.

As to me, I was thrown into some kind of daze at the moment when the door was opened and even forgot to fold my hands or bow my head. The first thing I recorded mentally was the fact that the statue was indeed thickly plated with gold, just as I had expected. My anticipation proved wrong in all other points apart from this, however. The statue of Buddha was so very different from the picture I had had in my mind before I saw it. First of all, it had an

그러한 어떤 가부좌상이었다.

내가 그것을 바라보는 순간부터 나는 미묘한 충격에 사로잡히게 되었다고 말했지만 그러나 그 미묘한 충격을 나는 어떠한 말로써도 표현할 길이 없다. 다만 나는 그것을 바라보고 있는 동안 처음 보았을 때 받은 그 경악과 충격이 점점 더 전율(戰慄)과 공포로 화하여 나를 후려갈기는 듯한 어지러움에 휩싸일 뿐이었다고나 할까. 곁에 있던 청운이 나의 얼굴을 돌아다보았을 때도 나는 손끝 하나 까딱하지 못하며 정강마루와 아래턱을 그냥 덜덜덜 떨고 있을 뿐이었다.

'저건 부처님이 아니다! 불상도 아니야!'

나는 나 자신도 모르는 사이에 이렇게 목이 터지도록 소리를 지르고 싶었으나 나의 목구멍은 얼어붙은 듯 아무런 말도 새어나지 않았다.

이튿날 새벽 예불을 마치고 내가 청운과 더불어 원혜대사에게 아침 인사를 드리러 갔을 때 스님은,

"어저께 금불각 구경을 갔었니?"

물었다.

내가 겁에 질린 얼굴로 참배했다고 대답하자, 스님은

incense-burner on the head. His hands were folded in the front. But his head drooped, back bent forward, and even his mouth was half open in a sloppy way. It was not the usual image of dignity, holiness and physical perfection. In short, the Buddha I saw was exceedingly shabby-looking. In addition, there was something about this Buddha that filled one with a nearly painful feeling of sympathy. It was a life size statue in the formal Kyŏlgabujwa (sitting in a certain formal style of Buddhist tradition) posture. As I looked on, I was more and more astounded that the image I saw before my eyes was so immeasurably different from the usual Buddha image: dignified, saintly and beautiful. What a pity-and-affection-drawing picture it was that I saw in front of my eyes! The sitting Buddha could not even sit with a straight back. And the expression on the face above which sat the incense-burner looked like it was crying at one glance but laughing at another. It seemed to grimace and then it looked as if it were agonizing in indescribable sorrow, suffering or pain. I began to feel something choking me in the chest as if to smother me. It was a statue of Buddha I had never once seen or heard of.

I said I was astounded by my first sight of the

꽤 만족한 얼굴로,

"불은이로다."

했다.

나는 맘속으로 그건 부처님이 아니었어요, 부처님의 상호가 아니었어요, 하고 소리를 지르고 싶은 충동을 깨달았으나 굳이 입을 닫치고 참을 수밖에 없었다.

이때 스님(원혜대사)은 내 맘속을 헤아리는 듯,

"그래 어느 부처님이 제일 맘에 들더냐?"

물었다.

나는 실상 그 등신불에 질려 그 곁에 모신 다른 불상들은 거의 살펴보지도 못했던 것이다.

"다른 부처님은 미처 보지도 못했어요. 가운데 모신 부, 부처님이 어떻게나 무, 무서운지……."

나는 또 아래턱이 덜덜덜 떨려 말을 이을 수 없었다.

원혜대사는 말없이 나의 얼굴(아래턱이 덜덜덜 떨리는)을 가만히 건너다보고만 있었다. 그러자 나는 지금 금방 내 입으로 부처님이라고 말한 것이 생각났다. 왜 그런지 그렇게 말해서는 안 될 것을 말한 듯한 야릇한 반발이 내 속에서 폭발되었다.

"그렇지만…… 아니었어요…… 부처님의 상호 같지

statue. But it is impossible for me to describe what exactly it was that shocked me so much. I only remember the fact that as I kept looking at the statue, the feeling of shock changed itself gradually into a feeling of fear and that I ended up feeling all shaken up as if something powerful had given me a violent beating. When Ch'ŏngun turned his head to me, I was bound in a state of complete immobility with the lower halves of my legs and my chin trembling as if in a fit.

(That is no Buddha! That is no statue of Buddha!)

Without knowing it, I was ardently wishing to shout these words at the top of my voice. My throat was blocked up, however, and I could produce no sound.

When I showed up in front of Master Wŏnhye after the morning prayers with Ch'ŏngun, next morning, the Master asked:

"Did you go to Kŭmbul-gak yesterday?"

When I answered in a fearful voice that I did indeed worship at the shrine, he said contentedly:

"It's Buddha's blessings."

I wanted to shout:

(It was no Buddha! He did not have the Buddha's face!)

But I kept my mouth shut.

않았어요."

나는 전신의 힘을 다하여 겨우 이렇게 말해 버렸다.

"왜, 머리에 얹은 것이 화관이 아니고 향로라서 그러니!……그렇지, 그건 향로야."

원혜대사는 조금도 나를 꾸짖는 빛이 아니었다. 오히려 나의 그러한 불만에 구미가 당기는 듯한 얼굴이었다.

"……."

나는 잠자코 원혜대사의 얼굴을 쳐다보고 있었다. 곁에 있던 청운이 두어 번이나 나에게 눈짓을 했을 만치 나의 두 눈은 스님을 쏘아보듯이 빛나고 있었다.

"자네 말대로 하면 부처님이 아니고 나한(羅漢)님이란 말인가. 그렇지만 나한님도 머리 위에 향로를 쓴 분은 없잖아. 오백 나한(五百羅漢) 중에도……."

나는 역시 입을 닫친 채 호기심에 가득 찬 눈으로 스님의 얼굴을 쳐다볼 뿐이었다.

그러나 원혜대사는 더 자세한 이야기를 들려주지 않았다.

"그렇지, 본래는 부처님이 아니야. 모두가 부처님이라고 부르게 됐어. 본래는 이 절 스님인데 성불(成佛)을 했

But the Master seemed to know what was in my mind. He said:

"Which Buddha did you like best?"

The fact was that, driven out of my wits at the sight of the golden statue, I had not had a chance to look at the other Buddhas in the shrine.

"I did not see other Buddhas. The Buddha in the center frightened me so much that I..."

At this point, my lower chin started trembling again and I could not continue with my words.

Master Wŏnhye looked at my face with the chin still trembling. Suddenly I remembered that I had just uttered the word Buddha referring to the fearful ugly statue. So I hurried to say as if I had uttered something I had no right to say:

"But no... No... It was not... It was not the face of a Buddha."

I said this summoning up all the strength that lay in me.

"Why? Is it because he has the incense-burner on his head instead of a wreath? It is really an incense-burner that he has on his head, isn't it?"

He did not sound reproachful. On the contrary, he seemed to be rather favorably interested in my reaction. I did not say anything further. Instead I

으니까 부처님이라고 부른 게지. 자네도 마찬가지야."

스님은 말을 마치고 가만히 두 손을 모아 합장을 한다.

나도 머리를 숙이며 합장을 올리고 자리에서 일어났다.

그날 아침 공양을 마치고 청정실로 건너올 때 청운은 나에게 턱으로 금불각 쪽을 가리키며,

"나도 첨엔 이상했어, 그렇지만 이 절에선 영검이 제일 많은 부처님이라오."

했다.

"영검이라고?"

나는 이렇게 물었지만 실상은 청운이 서슴지 않고 부처님이라고 부르는 말에 더욱 놀랐던 것이다. 조금 전에도 원혜대사로부터 '모두가 부처님이라고 부르게 됐다'는 말을 듣긴 했지만, 그때까지의 나의 머릿속에 박혀 있는 습관화된 개념으로써는 도저히 부처님과 스님을 혼동할 수 없었던 것이다.

"그럼, 그래서 그렇게 새전이 많다오."

청운의 대답이었다. 그는 계속해서 들려주었다.

stared into the Master's eyes steadily for so long that Ch'ŏngun gave me a warning sign with his eyes a couple of times.

"According to you, he is no Buddha but a Nahan (Buddha's disciple), maybe? But even a Nahan does not hold an incense-burner on his head. Not even among the Five-Hundred-Nahans is there any with an incense-burner on the head..."

I kept my silence and continued to stare at the Master, my mind full of curiosity.

But he did not seem inclined to go on.

"In a way, you are right. Because he was not a Buddha originally. It is just that everybody came to call him a Buddha. He was the father monk of this temple. Since he attained Buddhaship, everybody began to call him Buddha. You will, too."

After these words, the Master folded his hands together. I too folded my hands bowing my head at the same time and got up from my seat.

As I was returning to my room after the morning service, Ch'ŏngun caught up with me. Pointing toward Kŭmbul-gak with his chin, he said:

"I was puzzled at first like you. But he is the Buddha that has worked more miracles than any other Buddha in this temple."

……스님의 이름은 잘 모른다. 당(唐)나라 때다. 일천 수백 년 전이라고 한다. 소신공양(燒身供養)으로 성불을 했다. 공양을 드리고 있을 때 여러 가지 신이(神異)가 일어났다. 이것을 보고 들은 수많은 사람들이 구름같이 모여들어서 아낌없이 새전과 불공을 드렸는데 그들 가운데 영검을 보지 못한 사람은 하나도 없다. 그 뒤에도 계속해서 영검이 있었다. 지금까지 여기 금불각(등신금불)에 빌어서 아이를 낳고 병을 고치고 한 사람의 수효는 수천 수만을 헤아린다. 그 밖에도 소원을 성취한 사람은 이루 다 헤일 수가 없다…….

나도 청운에게서 소신공양이란 말을 들었을 때 몸이 부르르 떨렸다.

"그러면 그럴 테지."

나는 무슨 뜻인지 이렇게 중얼거렸다. 그리고 잇달아 눈을 감고 합장을 올렸다. 나무아미타불, 나무아미타불! 나의 입에서는 나도 모르게 염불이 흘러나왔다.

아아, 그 고뇌! 그 비원(悲願)! 나의 감은 두 눈에서는 눈물이 번져 나왔다. 나무아미타불, 나무아미타불! 나는 발작과도 같이 곧장 염불을 외웠다.

"나도 처음 봤을 때는 가슴이 뭉클했다오. 그 뒤에 여

"Miracles?"

I said as if surprised by the word. But in fact I was more surprised that Ch'ŏngun called the statue "Buddha" without any resistance of discomfort. Although it was only a while ago that Master Wŏnhye had told me that "everybody began to call him a Buddha," as yet the fixed idea about what a Buddha should look like that was nailed in my head was too strong to allow me to even begin considering the ungainly statue a Buddha. I could not take a monk for a Buddha, in short.

"Yes, miracles. That is why there's so much money offered at his shrine."

Ch'ŏngun said. And he continued:

Nobody knew the real name of the monk. It was during the T'ang dynasty in China, one thousand and several hundred years ago, that is. He attained Buddhaship by *sosin kongyang*. that is, by burning himself in offering. While the process of his self-offering devotion continued, many a miracle occurred. People who saw or heard of these miracles thronged to the temple and offered money and prayers profusely. None among them went home without receiving some miracle. The miracles happened afterward, too, and the number of people

러 번 보고 나니까 차츰 심상해지더군."

청운은 빙긋이 웃으며 나를 위로하듯이 말했다.

그것은 그렇다 하더라도 나에게는 아무래도 석연치 못한 것이 있다…….

소신공양으로 성불을 했다면 부처님이 되었어야 하지 않는가. 부처님이 되었다면 지금까지 모든 불상에서 보아온 바와 같은 거룩하고 원만하고 평화스러운 상호는 아니라 할지라도 그에 가까운 부처님다움은 있어야 하지 않을까. 거룩하고 부드럽고 평화스러운 맛은 지녔어야 하지 않겠는가. 그러나 금불각의 가부좌상은 어디까지나 인간을 벗어나지 못한 고뇌와 비원이 서린 듯한 얼굴이 아니던가. 그럼에도 불구하고 과거의 어떠한 대각(大覺)보다도 그렇게 영검이 많다는 것은 무슨 까닭인가.

나의 머릿속에서는 잠시도 이러한 의문들이 가셔지지 않았다. 더구나 청운에게서 소신공양으로 성불했다는 이야기를 들은 뒤부터는 금불이 아닌 새까만 숯덩이가 곧잘 눈에 삼삼거려 배길 수 없었다.

사흘 뒤에 나는 다시 금불을 찾았다. 사흘 전에 받은

who were given a child or had their sicknesses cured by praying at the shrine was numberless. There were thousands of other people who had wishes other than these fulfilled...

When I heard the word *sosin kongyang* from Ch'ŏngun's mouth, a shiver went through my body.

"That explains..." I said not fully realizing what it was I meant by these words. I closed my eyes and folded my hands in *hapjang*. Namuamit'abul, namuamit'abul, na-muamit'abul, my lips mumbled by themselves.

Oh that he should have gone through so much suffering and sorrows! The tears oozed out of my closed eyes. Namuamit'abul, namuamit'abul, I repeated impulsively.

"I too felt like crying at first. But as 1 kept on seeing him, I became more used to the Buddha."

Ch'ŏngun said with a smile as if to comfort me.

There was, however, still one point which was not clear to me. It was that if he had attained the Buddhaship through *sosin kongyang*, he should have come to look like a Buddha, the image of holiness, harmony, and peace. Even if he did not fit perfectly into this mold, shouldn't he at least come close to it? But there was nothing holy, harmonious, or

충격이 어쩌면 나의 병적인 환상의 소치가 아닐까 하는 마음과, 또 청운의 말대로 '여러 번' 봐서 '심상해'진다면 나의 가슴에 사무친 '오뇌와 비원'의 촉수(觸手)도 다소 무디어지리라는 생각에서였다.

문이 열리자, 나는 그날 청운이 하던 대로 이내 머리를 수그리며 합장을 올렸다. 입으로는 쉴 새 없이 나무아미타불을 부르며…… 눈까풀과 속눈썹이 바르르 떨리며 나의 눈이 열렸을 때 금불은 사흘 전의 그 모양 그대로 향로를 이고 앉아 있었다. 거룩하고 원만한 것의 상징인 듯한 부처님의 상호와는 너무나 거리가 먼, 우는 듯한, 웃는 듯한, 찡그린 듯한, 오뇌와 비원이 서린 듯한 가부좌상임에는 변함이 없었으나, 그 무어라고 형언할 수 없는 슬픔이랄까 아픔 같은 것이 전날처럼 송두리째 나의 가슴을 움켜잡는 듯한 전율에 휩쓸리지는 않았다. 나의 가슴은 이미 그러한 '슬픔이랄까 아픔 같은 것'으로 메워져 있었고, 또 그에게서 '거룩하고 원만한 것의 상징인 부처님의 상호'를 기대하는 마음은 가셔져 있었기 때문인지도 몰랐다.

나는 다시 눈을 감고 합장을 올리며, 입술이 바르르 떨리듯 오랫동안 아미타불을 부른 뒤 그 앞에서 물러났다.

peaceful about the sitting statue. It had too much of human agony and sorrow on the face. Then why is it that this particular Buddha works more wonders than many a holy man in the past who attained Buddhaship.

These questions stayed in my head and would not go away. Besides, after hearing about the way in which the monk had offered himself, that is, by *sosin kongyang*, I kept seeing the Buddha as a huge chunk of burnt coal.

Three days after, I visited the golden statue again. I had come to think that maybe it was because of a morbid state of mind that I experienced the kind of shock I had, or that if, as Ch'ŏngun suggested, I looked at the Buddha again, I might become less vulnerable to the sense of agony and sorrow emitted by the Buddha.

When the door opened, I bowed my head and folded my hands the way Ch'ŏngun did the first day. My mouth was uttering the invocation: Namuamit'abul repeatedly.

When finally I opened my eyes and looked at the Buddha, I found him sitting with the incense-burner on his head and in the same deep sorrow and suffering in which I had found him three days ago.

그날 저녁 예불을 마치고 청운과 더불어 원혜대사에게 저녁 인사(자리에 들기 전의)를 갔을 때 스님은 나를 보고,

"너 금불을 보고 나서 괴로워하는구나?"

했다.

"……."

나는 고개를 수그린 채 입을 열지 못하고 있었다.

"그럼, 너 금불각에 있는 그 불상의 기록을 봤느냐?"

스님이 또 물으시기에 내가 못 봤다고 했더니, 그러면 기록을 한번 보라고 했다.

이튿날 내가 청운과 더불어 아침 인사를 드릴 때 원혜대사는, 자기가 금불각에 일러두었으니 가서 기록을 청해서 보고 오라고 했다.

나는 스님께 합장하고 물러나와 곧 금불각으로 올라갔다. 금불각의 노승이 돌함[石函]에서 내준 폭이 한 뼘 남짓, 길이가 두 뼘가량 되는 책자를 받아들었을 때 향기가 코를 찌르는 듯했다(벌레를 막기 위한 향료인 듯). 두터운 표지 위에는 금 글씨로 '만적선사소신성불기(萬寂禪師燒身成佛記)'라 씌어 있고, 책 모서리에도 금물이 먹여져 있었다.

Again, I could not find a trace of holiness, or peace about him. Unlike the previous occasion, however, I did not experience the acute sadness or feeling of pity for the Buddha this time. Maybe it was because my mind was already burdened with sadness and pity, and also had stopped expecting to find the usual attributed of a Buddha—holiness, harmony and peace— in him.

I closed my eyes again and, folding my hands, repeated "Namiamit'abul" until my lips trembled from exhaustion.

When I appeared, after the evening service, in front of Master Wŏnhye to offer him evening greetings with Ch'ŏngun, the Master said;

"You are suffering because of the golden Buddha, aren't you?"

I bowed my head but did not say anything.

"Did you read the records on the golden Buddha that is in Kŭmbul-gak?" asked the Master again.

I answered him that I had not read it. He told me to find a chance to read it, then.

Next morning, when I went to offer him morning greetings along with Ch'ŏngun, he said that he had given words to the people at Kŭmbul-gak to allow me to look at the record when I should come there.

표지를 젖히자 지면은 모두 잿빛 바탕(물감을 먹인 듯)이요, 그 위에 사연은 금 글씨로 다음과 같이 씌어져 있었다.

萬寂法名俗名曰耆姓曹氏也金陵出生父未詳母張氏改嫁謝公仇之家仇有一子名曰信前室之所生也年似與耆各十有餘歲一日母給食于二兒秘置以毒信之食耆偶窺之而按是母貪謝家之財爲我故謀害前室之子以如此耆不堪悲懷乃自欲將取信之食母見之驚而失色奪之曰是非汝之食也何取信之食耶信與耆默而不答數日後信去自家行蹟渺然耆曰信已去家我必携與信而然後歸家卽以隱身而爲僧改稱萬寂以此爲法名住於金陵法林院後移淨願寺無風庵修法于海覺禪師寂二十四歲之春曰我生非大覺之材不如供養吾身以報佛恩乃燒身而供養佛前時忽降雨沛然不犯寂之燒身寂光漸明忽縣圓光以如月輪會衆見之而震撼佛恩癒身病衆曰是寂之法力所致競擲私財賽錢多積以賽鍍金寂之燒身拜之爲佛然後奉置于金佛閣時唐中宗十六年聖曆二年三月朔日.

만적은 법명이요, 속명은 기, 성은 조씨다. 금릉서 났지만 아버지가 어떤 이인지는 잘 모른다. 어머니 장씨

I folded my hands and bowed. After leaving his presence, I left right away for Kŭmbul-gak. The old monk at the shrine opened a stone chest and out of it picked up a booklet about five inches wide and ten inches long. As he handed me the booklet, I noticed that there was a strong smell of incense on the booklet. (It must have been a preventive against bugs.) On the thick cover of the booklet was written in gold: The Record of Monk Manjŏk's Attaining Buddhaship Through *sosin kongyang*. The four corners of the cover were also decorated in gold.

When I opened the book on the first page, I found out that the paper that was used was grey in color (it had probably been dyed this color). The writing itself was done in golden paint. I read:

萬寂法名俗名曰耆姓曹氏也金陵出生父未詳母張氏改嫁謝公仇之家仇有一子名曰信前室之所生也年似與耆各十有餘歲一日母給食于二兒秘置以毒信之食耆偶窺之而按是母貪謝家之財爲我故謀害前室之子以如此耆不堪悲懷乃自欲將取信之食母見之驚而失色奪之曰是非汝之食也何取信之食耶信與耆默而不答數日後信去自家行蹟渺然耆曰信已去家我必携與信而然後歸家卽以隱身而爲僧改稱萬寂以此爲法名住於金陵法林院後移淨願寺無風庵修法于海覺禪師寂二十四歲之春曰我生非大覺之材不如

는 사구(謝仇)라는 사람에게 개가를 했는데 사구에게 한 아들이 있어 이름을 신이라 했다. 나이는 기와 같은 또래로 모두가 여남은 살씩 되었다. 하루는 어미(장씨)가 두 아이에게 밥을 주는데 가만히 독약을 신의 밥에 감추었다. 기가 우연히 이것을 엿보게 되었는데, 혼자 생각하기를 이는 어머니가 나를 위하여 사씨 집의 재산을 탐냄으로써 전실 자식인 신을 없애려고 하는 짓이라 하였다. 기가 슬픈 맘을 참지 못하여 스스로 신의 밥을 제가 먹으려 할 때 어머니가 보고 크게 놀라 질색을 하며 그것을 뺏고 말하기를 이것은 너의 밥이 아니다. 어째서 신의 밥을 먹느냐 했다. 신과 기는 아무도 대답을 하지 않았다. 며칠 뒤 신이 자기 집을 떠나서 자취를 감춰 버렸다. 기가 말하기를 신이 이미 집을 나갔으니 내가 반드시 찾아 데리고 돌아오리라 하고 곧 몸을 감추어 중이 되고 이름을 만적이라 고쳤다. 처음은 금릉에 있는 법림원에 있다가 나중은 정원사 무풍암으로 옮겨서, 거기서 해각선사에게 법을 배웠다. 만적이 스물네 살 되던 해 봄에, 나는 본래 도(道)를 크게 깨칠 인재가 못 되니, 내 몸을 이대로 공양하여 부처님의 은혜에 보답함과 같지 못하다 하고 몸을 태워 부처님 앞에 바치

供養吾身以報佛恩乃燒身而供養佛前時忽降雨沛然不犯寂之燒身寂光漸明忽縣圓光以如月輪會衆見之而震撼佛恩癒身病衆曰是寂之法力所致競擲私財賽錢多積以賽鍍金寂之燒身拜之爲佛然後奉置于金佛閣時唐中宗十六年聖曆二年三月朔日.

(Manjŏk is his sacred name. His worldly name is Ki and his family name is Cho. He was born in Kŭmrŭng but nothing is known about his father. His mother, Chang by name, was remarried to a man named Sa-Ku and gave birth to a son whom they named Sin. In age he was close to Ki. They were a little over ten years old each when an incident happened in the house where they all lived together. One day. their mother put poison in Sin's rice bowl when serving the tray to the two boys. Ki happened to see this and judged that his mother was doing this to take away the property of the Sa house so that her other son, Ki, that is, could take advantage of it. This thought plunged Ki into sadness, and picking up Sin's rice bowl, he started to eat from it. His mother saw this, however, and snatching the bowl from him in fright, scolded him saying it was wrong that he should eat what belonged to his brother. Neither of the boys said anything. A few days after, Sin disappeared from the house. Ki said he would go after Sin and bring him home. But he never went back. He became a monk and was given the sacred name Manjŏk. He

는데 그때 마침 비가 쏟아졌으나 만적의 타는 몸을 적시지 못할 뿐 아니라 점점 더 불빛이 환하더니 홀연히 보름달 같은 원광이 비쳤다. 모인 사람들이 이것을 보고 크게 불은을 느끼고 모두가 제 몸의 병을 고치니 무리들이 말하기를 이는 만적의 법력 소치라 하고 다투어 사재를 던져 새전이 많이 쌓여졌다. 새전으로써 만적의 탄 몸에 금을 입히고 절하여 부처님이라 하였다. 그 뒤에 금불각에 모시니 때는 당나라 중종 십육년 성력(연호) 이년 삼월 초하루다.

내가 이 기록을 다 읽고 나서 청정실로 돌아가니 원혜대사가 나를 불렀다.

"기록을 보고 나니 괴롬이 덜 하냐?"

스님이 물었다.

"처음같이 무섭지는 않았습니다마는 그 괴롭고 슬픈 빛은 가셔지지 않았습니다."

내가 대답하자, 스님은 고개를 끄덕이며,

"당연한 일이야, 기록이 너무 간략하고 섬소(纖疎)[4]해서……."

했다. 그것이 자기는 그보다 훨씬 많은 것을 알고 있는

served at a temple in Nanking called Pŏprimwŏn, but later moved to the little temple Mup'ung-am that belonged to Chŏngwŏn-sa and studied Buddhism under Master Haegak. At the age of twenty-four, Manjŏk proclaimed that since he did not have the endowments for a great awakening, he would offer himself in *sosin kongyang* and thus serve Buddha's way. As he was burning himself, there poured a heavy rain but the rain could not wet Manjŏk's body or extinguish the fire that was burning him. Instead the flame grew bigger and then suddenly people saw a halo the shape and hue of a full moon formed around his head. The people who were gathered there felt the blessing of the Buddha deeply and all who had any illness got it cured. They said that it was the spiritual power emanating from Manjŏk's body and offered huge sums of money. The monks covered the burnt body of Manjŏk with gold with the money the believers offered up in a pile and called it "Buddha." This Buddha was later installed in Kŭmbul-gak. It was the first day of March in the sixteenth year of the reign of Chungtsung, T'ang.)

When I returned to Ch'ŏngjŏngsil after reading this record. Master Wŏnhye called me.

"Did you feel more comfortable after reading the record?" He asked.

"I felt less scared. But I still found sadness and

듯한 말씨였다.

"그렇지만 천이백 년도 넘는 옛날 일인데 기록 이외에 다른 일을 어떻게 알겠습니까?"

또 내가 물었다.

이에 대하여 원혜대사는 전해 내려오는 이야기가 있는데, 산(절)에서는 그것을 함부로 이야기하지 않는 것으로 알고 있으며, 그러니까 그만큼 금불각의 등신불에 대해서는 모두들 그 영검을 두려워하고 있는 셈이라고 정색을 하고 말했다.

원혜대사가 나에게 들려준 이야기는 다음과 같다. 이것은 물론 천이백 년간 등신금불에 대하여 절에서 내려오는 이야기를 원혜대사가 정리해서 간단히 한 이야기다.

……만적이 중이 되기까지의 이야기는 대개 기록과 같다. 그러나 그가 자기 몸을 불살라서 부처님께 공양을 올린 동기에 대해서는 전해 오는 다른 이야기가 몇 있다. 그것을 차례에 좇아 이야기하면 다음과 같다.

만적이 처음 금릉 법림원에서 중이 되었는데 그때 그를 거두어준 스님에 취뢰(吹籟)라는 중이 있었다. 그 절

pain on his face," I answered.

The Master nodded his head once or twice and said:

"It is only natural. The record is too brief and incomplete..."

He seemed to know more than was recorded.

"But it is something that happened over twelve hundred years ago. How could anything be known except what is in the record?" I asked him.

Master Wŏnhye told me that there were stories that have been handed down among monks. He said, however, that it was a general rule among them not to discuss these without good reasons. Maybe, it was out of deference for the miracle-working power of the Buddha, he said.

What Master Wŏnhye subsequently told me is roughly as follows. This was of course a concoction of many stories edited into one tolerably systematic story by Master Wŏnhye.

The story up to the time when Manjŏk became a monk is about the same as in the record. But there seemed to be several versions of the motive from which he made up his mind to offer himself to the Buddha's way by self-burning. The story I heard from Master Wŏnhye runs as follows.

의 공양을 맡아 있는 공양주(供養主) 스님이었다. 만적은 취뢰스님의 상좌로 있으면서 불법을 배우기 시작했다. 그러니까 취뢰스님이 그에 대한 일체를 돌보아준 것이다.

만적이 열여덟 살 때—그러니까 그가 법림원에 들어온 지 오 년 뒤—취뢰스님이 열반(涅槃)하시게 되자 만적은 스님(취뢰)의 은공을 갚기 위하여 자기 몸을 불전에 헌신할 결의를 했다.

만적이 그 뜻을 법사(법림원의) 운봉선사(雲峰禪師)에게 아뢰자 운봉선사는 만적의 그릇[器]됨을 보고 더 수도를 계속하도록 타이르며 사신(捨身)을 허락하지 않았다.

만적이 정원사의 무풍암에 해각선사를 찾았다는 것도 운봉선사의 알선에 의한 것이다. 그가 해각선사 밑에서 지낸 오 년간의 수도 생활이란 뼈를 깎고 살을 가는 정진이었으나 법력의 경지는 짐작할 길이 없다.

만적이 스물세 살 나던 해 겨울에 금릉 방면으로 나갔다가 전날의 사신(謝信)을 만났다. 열세 살 때 자기 어머니의 모해를 피하여 집을 나간 사신이었다. 그리고 자기는 이 사신을 찾아 역시 집을 나왔다가 그를 찾지

When Manjŏk first became a monk at Pŏprimwŏn in Nanking, there was an older monk named Ch'wiroe who took care of Manjŏk. He was the Master of *kong-yang* (offering) at the temple. Manjŏk was his head disciple learning Buddhist doctrines from him.

When Manjŏk became eighteen, that is five years after he came to Pŏprimwŏn, Ch'wiroe died. In order to repay his kindness, Manjŏk decided to give up his body to the altar of the Buddha.

When Manjŏk told Unbong, the Zen priest at Pŏprimwŏn, however, he discouraged Manjŏk from his determination for a *sosin* (the practice of giving oneself up to Buddha by mutilating one's body so that he may devote himself the more completely to Buddha) because he could see that Manjŏk had a capacity for a bigger service to Buddhism.

It was by recommendation of Unbong that Manjŏk sought Master Haegak, another Zen priest, at Mup'ung-am of Chŏngwŏn-sa. For five years, he studied and trained under Haegak in a most persevering and painstaking self-discipline. How great his sacred power had grown cannot be fathommed.

When Manjŏk was twenty-three years old, he had an occasion to go near Nanking, and, while there, ran into Sa-Sin, the brother of his former days, who

못하고 중이 된 채 어느덧 꼭 십 년 만에 그를 다시 만난 것이다. 그러나 그때 다시 만난 사신을 보고는 비록 속세의 인연을 끊어버린 만적으로서도 한줄기 눈물을 금할 수 없었던 것이다. 착하고 어질던 사신이 어쩌면 하늘의 형벌을 받았단 말인고. 사신은 문둥병이 들어 있었던 것이다.

만적은 자기의 목에 걸었던 염주를 벗겨서 사신의 목에 걸어주고 그 길로 곧장 정원사로 돌아왔다.

그때부터 만적은 화식(火食)을 끊고 말을 잃었다. 이듬해 봄까지 그가 먹은 것은 하루에 깨 한 접시뿐이었다(그때까지의 목욕 재계는 말할 것도 없다).

이듬해 이월 초하룻날 그는 법사 스님(운봉선사)과 공양주 스님 두 분만을 모시고 취단식(就壇式)을 봉행했다. 먼저 법의를 벗고 알몸이 된 뒤에 가늘고 깨끗한 명주를 발끝에서 어깨까지(목 위만 남겨놓고) 전신에 감았다. 그러고는 단 위에 올라가 가부좌(跏趺坐)를 개고 앉자 두 손을 모아 합장을 올렸다. 그리하여 그가 염불을 외우기 시작하는 것과 동시에 곁에서 들기름 항아리를 받들고 서 있던 공양주 스님이 그의 어깨에서부터 기름을 들어 부었다.

had left the house fleeing from their mother's murderous intrigue. Manjŏk himself had left the house in search of Sa-Sin, but instead of finding him, had become a monk. Now he was seeing him after ten years. But what a re-encounter it was! Although Manjŏk was now delivered of worldly thoughts and sentiments, he could not help feeling a heart-wringing sorrow at seeing his half brother after so many years. It was because Sa-Sin who had been good and gentle as a child had become a leper, the worst punishment one can receive from heaven!

Manjŏk took off the beads from his own neck and hung it round Sa-Sin's and returned to his temple right away.

From then on, Manjŏk stopped eating any cooked food and until next spring, all he ate a day was a dish of sesame seeds. (No need to mention his performing ablution most faithfully during this period).

On the first day of February next year, he performed the *Ch'witan-sik*, ceremony of mounting the altar attended only by the Zen pirest Unbong and another elder monk, the Master of Offering. First, he took off his clothes. His naked body was then bound with thin strips of clean white silk from the tips of his feet to the shoulders (leaving only his head

기름을 다 붓고, 취단식이 끝나자 법사 스님과 공양주 스님은 합장을 올리고 그 곁을 떠났다.

기름에 결은 만적은 그때부터 한 달 동안(삼월 초하루까지) 단 위에서 움직이지 않았다. 가부좌를 갠 채, 합장을 한 채, 숨 쉬는 화석이 되어가고 있었다.

이레에 한 번씩 공양주 스님이 들기름 항아리를 안고 장막(帳幕—흰 천으로 장막을 치고 있었다) 안으로 들어오면 어깨에서부터 다시 기름을 부어주고 돌아가는 일밖에 그 누구도 이 장막 안을 엿보지 못했다.

이렇게 한 달이 찬 뒤, 이날의 성스러운 불공에 참여하기 위하여 산중의 스님들은 물론이요, 원근 각처의 선남선녀들이 모여들어, 정원사 법당 앞 넓은 뜰을 메웠다.

대공양(大供養 : 소신공양을 가리킴)은 오시 초에 장막이 걷히면서부터 시작되었다. 오백을 헤아리는 승려가 단을 향해 합장을 하고 선 가운데 공양주 스님이 불 담긴 향로를 받들고 단 앞으로 나아가 만적의 머리 위에 얹었다. 그와 동시 그 앞에 합장하고 선 승려들의 입에서 일제히 아미타불이 불려지기 시작했다.

만적의 머리 위에 화관같이 씌워진 향로에서는 점점

from the neck upwards). He mounted the altar then and sat in the *kabujwa* position folding his hands in the front. At the same time as he started chanting prayes, the Master of Offering started pouring oil from a jug he was holding in his hands.

When all the oil was poured and the ceremony ended, the two elder monks folded their hands in *hapjang* and left the place.

Oil-soaked, Manjŏk stayed like that for one full month (until the first of March). He was turning into a live fossil in his *kabujwa* position folding his hands in *hapjang*.

Once in seven days, the Master of Offering came with his jug of wild sesame oil and entered through the curtains which had been hung to keep Manjŏk in separation unseen by anybody. The Master of Offering poured the oil down from Manjŏk's shoulders and went back after all the oil was poured.

When one full month was spent like this it was time for the sacred service to take place. In order to take part in this special service, a horde of believers, not to speak of all the monks in the mountain, gathered from around the area. The spacious courtyard in front of the main hall of Chŏngwŏn-sa filled with the crowd that day.

더 많은 연기가 오르기 시작했다. 이미 오랜 동안의 정진으로 말미암아 거의 화석이 되어가고 있던 만적의 육신이지만, 불기운이 그의 숨골(정수리)을 뚫었을 때는 저절로 몸이 움칠해졌다. 그리하여 그때부터 눈에 보이지 않게 그의 고개와 등, 가슴이 조금씩 앞으로 숙여져 갔다.

들기름에 결은 만적의 육신이 연기로 화하여 나가는 시간은 길었다. 그러나 그 앞에 선 오백의 대중(승려)은 아무도 쉬지 않고 아미타불을 불렀다.

신시(申時)[5] 말(末)에 갑자기 비가 쏟아졌다. 그러나 웬일인지 단 위에는 비가 내리지 않았다. 만적의 머리 위로는 더 많은 연기가 오르기 시작했다.

염불을 올리던 중들과 그 뒤에서 구경하던 신도들이 신기한 일이라고 눈이 휘둥그레져서 만적을 바라보았을 때 그의 머리 뒤에는 보름달 같은 원광이 씌워져 있었다.

이때부터 새전이 쏟아지기 시작하여 그 뒤 삼 년간이나 그칠 날이 없었다.

이 새전으로 만적의 타다가 굳어진 몸에 금을 씌우고 금불각을 짓고 석대를 쌓았다…….

The Great *Kongyang* (*sosin kongyang*) started at the beginning of the Seventh Hour (from 11 a.m. to 1 p.m.) when the white curtains were drawn away. Five hundred monks stood facing the altar folding their hands in *hapjang*. The Master of Offering came out with an incense-burner with burning coals in them and drawing up to the altar, put it on Manjŏk's head. At the same time as he did this, all the monks who were standing with folded hands started chanting.

From the incense-burner that had been put on Manjŏk's head as if it were a wreath of flowers, smoke rose thicker and more profusely as the minutes passed. When the coal heat reached his breath pith, his body twitched involuntarily in spite of the fact that the long period of purification had turned him into a half fossil by this time. From this point on, his head and upper half of body bent forward little by little almost imperceptibly.

Manjŏk's body soaked in the oil of wild sesame seeds took long to be consumed into smoke. The five hundred monks, however, never ceased their chanting even once during the whole time.

At the end of the Ninth Hour, there was a sudden downpour of rain. But strangely enough, the rain did not fall on the altar on which Manjŏk sat, and in

원혜대사의 이야기를 듣고 있는 동안 나는 맘속으로 이렇게 해서 된 불상이라면 과연 지금의 저 금불각의 등신금불같이 될 수밖에 없으리란 생각이 들었다. 그리고 많은 부처님(불상) 가운데서 그렇게 인간의 고뇌와 슬픔을 아로새긴 부처님(등신불)이 한 분쯤 있는 것도 무방한 일일 듯했다.

그러나 이야기를 다 마치고 난 원혜대사는 이제 다시 나에게 그런 것을 묻지는 않았다.

"자네 바른손 식지를 들어보게."

했다.

이것은 지금까지 그가 이야기해 오던 금불각이나 등신불이나 만적의 소신공양과는 아무런 상관도 없는 엉뚱한 이야기가 아닐 수 없었다.

나는 달포 전에 남경 교외에서 진기수 씨에게 혈서를 바치느라고 내 입으로 살을 물어 떼었던 나의 식지를 쳐들었다.

그러나 원혜대사는 가만히 그것을 바라보고 있을 뿐 더 말이 없다. 왜 그 손가락을 들어 보이라고 했는지, 이 손가락과 만적의 소신공양이 무슨 관계가 있다는 겐지, 이제 그만 손을 내려도 좋다는 겐지 일절 뒷말이 없는

fact, more smoke rose from his head into the sky.

The monks and the believers were all astounded by this and did not know what to think. When they turned their eyes back to Manjŏk, however, they saw that there was a moonlike halo at the back of his head.

Money in offering poured in from that day and did not cease for three whole years.

The monks plated Manjŏk's body which had settled into a complete fossil in its half burnt state with gold using the money that came in and had the shrine, Kŭmbul-gak and the stone terrace built for it...

While I listened to this story, I told myself that if this was how the golden Buddha came into being, it was natural for it to look just like the golden Buddha, Tŭngsin-bul that I saw within Kŭmbul-gak. I also thought that it was perhaps proper that there was one Buddha among so many who showed so vividly the sorrow and pains of human life.

But Master Wŏnhye did not draw me back to the story of Manjŏk. He asked instead:

"Would you show me the index finger of your right hand?"

This was so sudden and so unrelated to anything

것이다.

"……."

"……."

태허루에서 정오를 아뢰는 큰 북소리가 목어(木魚)와 어우러져 으르렁거리며 들려온다.

1) 골짜기에서 흐르는 물.
2) 풀숲(풀이 무성한 수풀).
3) '열쇠'의 방언.
4) 체격이나 구조가 가냘프고 어설픔.
5) 오후 세 시에서 다섯 시까지.

* 작가 고유의 문체나 당시 쓰이던 용어를 그대로 살려 원문에 최대한 가깝게 표기하고자 하였다. 단, 현재 쓰이지 않는 말이나 띄어쓰기는 현행 맞춤법에 맞게 표기하였다.

* 이 책의 한국어판 저작권은 사단법인 한국문예학술저작권협회로부터 저작물의 사용 허락에 대한 동의를 받았다.

《사상계(思想界)》, 1961

we had been talking about—Kŭmbul-gak, Tŭngsin-bul, Manjŏk's *sosin kongyang*, etc.—that I was bewildered for a second. I showed him, however, the finger which I had bitten to write the characters in blood to present to Mr. Chin Ki-su more than a month ago.

Master Wŏnhye merely looked at it but did not say anything. He did not tell me why he asked me to show him the finger, what relation it had with the story of Manjŏk, or even whether I was now allowed to put my finger down. None of us spoke.

The big drum and the *mok-ŏ* (a kind of wooden drum in Buddhist temples) were sounding from T'aehŏru to announce midday.

* English translation first published in the July issue of *KOREA JOURNAL* 21:7 (Korean National Commission for UNESCO, 1981).

Translated by Sŏl Sun-bong

해설

Afterword

완벽한 대칭성의 세계에 이르는 도정

이경재 (문학평론가)

김동리는 가장 한국적인 작가이다. 그는 한국의 고유한 풍속과 사고를 형상화하는 데 발군의 실력을 발휘하였다. 그는 한국인의 정신적 탯줄이라 할 수 있는 무속이나 불교 등을 문학화하는 데 비범한 능력을 보여주었는데, 「등신불」(《사상계》, 1961)은 김동리의 불교적 세계관을 가장 잘 드러내면서, 동시에 예술적 품격을 유지하고 있는 명작이다. 불교는 종교이면서도 유일하게 야생의 사고와 공통의 지반에 서서 '대칭성의 사고'를 발달시켜 왔다. 이 대칭성의 사고는 인간과 인간, 인간과 자연 사이의 연속성과 동일성을 강조하는 사고를 말한다. 이러한 대칭성에 바탕하여 불교는 "자기와 타자의

The Process of Attaining the World of Perfect Symmetry

Lee Kyung-jae (literary critic)

Kim Tong-ni is one of *the* most characteristically Korean authors. He did an unparalleled job of depicting indigenous Korean customs and thought, especially shamanism and Buddhism. "Tŭngsin-bul," originally published in the November 1961 issue of *Sasang-gye*, is an excellent representation of Kim's Buddhist worldview, while at the same time preserving the work's artistic character.

Buddhism is the only religion that has developed a "symmetrical" way of thinking, as Nakazawa Shinichi argues in his book *Anthropology of Symmetry*. By symmetrical way of thinking Nakazawa means thought that emphasizes continuity and identity be-

구별이 없고 개념에 의한 세계의 분리도 없으며, 온갖 사물이 교환의 고리를 탈출한 증여의 공간에서 교류하는, 바로 그것이 무망상, 즉 망상이 없는 상태"(나카자와 신이치, 김옥희 역(2005), 「완성된 무의식—불교(1)」, 『대칭성 인류학』, 동아시아, 183쪽)라고 생각하는 종교이다. 본고에서는 대칭성이라는 개념을 중심으로 하여 김동리의 「등신불」을 살펴볼 것이다.

이 작품의 한복판에는 정원사의 금불각 속에 안치된 등신불이 놓여 있는데, 이 등신불을 보고, '나'는 두 번이나 "저건 부처님도 아니다! 불상도 아니야!"라고 외칠 정도로 큰 충격을 받는다. 이토록 '나'가 등신불을 보고 충격에 빠져 그 신성을 부인하려는 이유는, 등신불이 인간적인 특징을 너무나 많이 지니고 있기 때문이다. 아름답고 거룩하고 존엄성 있는 그러한 불상과는 달리, "허리도 제대로 펴고 앉지 못한, 머리 위에 조그만 향로를 얹은 채 우는 듯한, 웃는 듯한, 찡그린 듯한, 오뇌와 비원이 서린 듯한" 인간적 모습이 그 등신불을 부인하게 만드는 것이다. '내'가 경험하는 충격은 대부분의 종교가 신과 인간 사이에 비대칭적인 관계를 설정하는 것과 달리 불교는 신과 인간 사이에 대칭성의 사고를 작

tween human beings and nature. According to him, the ideal state in Buddhism is a "state without delusion," which he defines as "the state in which the self and the other are not distinguished, no notion divides the world, and all things interact within the space of giving, a space outside of exchanges." "Tŭngsin-bul" embodies this concept.

In the center of this story is a statue of Buddha, called Tŭngsin-bul, in the Kŭmbul-gak building of Chŏng-wŏnsa Temple. The first-person narrator is so shocked by this statue when he first sees it that he wants to shout out, "That is no Buddha! That is no statue of Buddha!" He is so shocked because the statue has too many human characteristics to be divine. In contrast to other "dignified, saintly, and beautiful" statues of Buddha, this one is described thusly: "The sitting Buddha could not even sit with a straight back. And the expression on the face above which sat the incense-burner looked like it was crying at one glance, but laughing at another. It seemed to grimace and then it looked as if it were agonizing in indescribable sorrow, suffering or pain." The narrator is shocked because of its symmetrical view of the relationship between Buddha and human beings in this Buddhism statue, unlike

동시키는 것에서 비롯된다. '내'가 신과 인간 사이의 대칭성을 구체적인 형상으로 드러낸 등신불 앞에서 그토록 당황하는 것은 "습관화된 개념으로써는 도저히 부처님과 스님을 혼동할 수 없는 것"이라고 밝힌 것에서 알 수 있듯이, 비대칭적인 사고에 익숙한 존재이기 때문이다.

「등신불」에서 만적이 등신불이 되어가는 과정은 전형적인 성불의 과정인 대신에 비대칭성의 사고를 벗어나 완벽한 대칭성의 세계에 이르는 과정이기도 하다. 등신불이 된 만적의 어머니는 비대칭적인 사고를 전형적으로 보여주는 인물이다. 그녀는 일찍 남편을 여의자, 아들인 만적을 데리고 사구라는 사람에게 개가를 한다. 사구에게는 신이라는 아들이 있었는데, 사씨 집의 재산을 탐낸 만적의 어머니는 신의 밥에 독약을 감추었다. 이 일로 신은 집을 나가고, 신을 찾아 나선 만적은 결국 출가를 하게 된 것이다. 만적의 어머니는 만적과 사신을, 자신이 낳은 아들과 다른 여인이 낳은 아들을 이토록 철저히 구별하는 분별심에 사로잡힌 여인이었던 것이다. 일단 등신불이 되기 위해서는 비대칭적 사고의 인격적 구현자라고 할 수 있는 어머니와의 결별

most other religious statues, which posit an asymmetrical relationship between God and human beings. This shock originates from the fact that the narrator is accustomed to an asymmetrical view of religion.

The process in which Manjŏk becomes the Tŭngsin-bul is simultaneously the process of his achieving Buddhahood and of his arriving at the state of perfect symmetry after denouncing an asymmetrical view. Manjŏk's mother holds a typically asymmetrical view of the world. A widow, she marries Sa-Ku, taking her son Manjŏk with her. Sa-Ku has a son named Sin. Wanting to take the Sa family estate from Sin and give it to Manjŏk, Manjŏk's mother puts poison into Sin's rice bowl. Although Manjŏk prevents Sin from dying, Sin disappears from the house a few days later. Manjŏk leaves home to look for Sin, and eventually becomes a Buddhist monk. In this episode, Manjŏk's mother reveals her asymmetrical view of the world in differentiation with her son Majŏk and her husband's son Sin. As a result, Manjŏk distances himself from his mother.

In the next stage, Manjŏk wants to do *sosin kongyang*, the practice of giving oneself to Buddha by

이 필요하다.

다음 단계로 만적은 자신을 거두어준 취뢰 스님이 열반하였을 때, 취뢰 스님의 은공을 갚기 위하여 소신공양을 시도한다. 그러나 이때 운봉 선사는 "만적의 그릇(器)됨을 보고 더 수도를 계속"하라며 소신공양을 허락하지 않는다. 과연 당대의 선사인 운봉은 왜 만적에게 소신공양을 허락하지 않은 것일까? 이것은 만적이 온전한 깨달음(대칭성)을 얻지 못했기 때문이다. 대승불교에서 깨달은 자를 의미하는 보살(bodhisattva)은 대칭성의 논리를 극한까지 밀어붙인 자이다. 순수한 증여가 사물의 증여로서 이루어질 때 어떤 식으로 이루어져야 하는지를 『금강반야경』에서는 "위대한 보살은 이와 같이 '누가 누구에게 무엇을'이라는 세 가지 생각조차 떨쳐버리고 보시해야 한다"라고 밝히고 있다. 불교에서 말하는 보시는 증여의 가장 순수한 형태를 말하고, 이는 대칭성의 논리를 실현하는 행위에 해당한다. 순수한 증여가 이루어지기 위해서는 '누가', '누구에게', '무엇을'이라는 세 가지 요소가 존재해서는 안 된다. 어느 하나라도 존재할 경우, 그것은 순수한 증여도 아니며 대칭성의 사고일 수도 없다. 첫 번째 소신공양에는 '만적이',

mutilating one's body, in order to repay his late master Ch'wiroe's kindness. However, the monk Unbong discourages Manjŏk from this path because he sees that "Manjŏk [has] a capacity for a bigger service to Buddha." Why does Unbong dissuade him from *sosin kongyang*? Because Manjŏk hasn't yet attained the state of complete awakening (or complete symmetry). In Mahayanist Buddhism, a bodhisattva is someone who pursues the logic of symmetry to its utmost. According to *The Diamond Sutra*, in order to give something in the pure sense of the word to someone, a great bodhisattva forgets about "who" gives "whom" and "what." In Buddhism, alms are the purest form of giving, and it is an act of putting the logic of symmetry into practice. If one wants to give in this pure sense, one must forget these distinctions. However, during the first attempt by Manjŏk at *sosin kongyang*, these three elements are still present, because it is an act of giving himself to Monk Ch'wiroe.

When Manjŏk wants to carry out *sosin kongyang* a second time, Monk Unbong allows it. In the meantime, Manjŏk has gone through ascetic practices for a long time, and met Sa-sin, now a Hansen's disease patient. When he meets Sa-sin, he gives his

'취뢰 스님에게', '자신의 몸'을 바친다는 세 가지 요소가 모두 존재했던 것이다.

만적이 두 번째 소신공양을 하겠다고 했을 때, 운봉 선사는 그제야 허락을 한다. 그 사이에 만적은 오 년 동안 수행(修行)을 했고, 스물세 살 되던 겨울에 금릉 방면으로 나갔다가 문둥병이 든 사신을 만났다. 이때 만적은 자신의 염주를 벗어서 사신의 목에 걸어주고, 정원사로 돌아온 것이다. 이것은 상징적인 차원에서 자신을 버린 행동에 해당한다고 볼 수 있다. 따라서 두 번째 소신공양에서는 '누가', '누구에게', '무엇을'이라는 세 가지 요소가 사라진 것이다. 이때에야 순수한 증여이자 대칭성 사고의 구현으로서의 소신공양은 이루어지게 된다.

작품의 마지막에 원혜대사는 '나'를 향해 "자네 바른 손 식지를 들어보게"라고 말한다. 이 일을 두고 '나'는 두 번이나 "만적의 소신공양과는 아무런 상관도 없는 엉뚱한 이야기"라거나 "이 손가락과 만적의 소신공양과 무슨 관계가 있다는 겐지"라고 의문을 표시한다. 이처럼 과도하게 두 사건의 무관함을 강조하는 것은 오히려 두 가지 사건이 깊이 연관되어 있음을 암시한다. 그 바른 손 식지에는 자신의 목숨을 살리기 위해 진기수 씨에게

meditation beads to him and returns to the temple. This is obviously a symbolic act of giving himself to someone else. In this act, the three elements of "who," "whom," and "what" disappear. Only then does he attain *sosin kongyang*, the embodiment of symmetrical thought.

At the end of the story, Master Wŏnhye asks the narrator to "show [him] the index finger of [his] right hand." The narrator is surprised because he believes that this act has nothing to do with "Manjŏk's *sosin kongyang*." However, this negation of the relationship between the two also suggests that they might be deeply related. There is a scar in the finger from the narrator biting it in order to write a letter in blood for Chin Kisu. This act of self-sacrifice corresponds to the second stage of Manjŏk's awakening. By asking him to show his finger, Monk Wŏnhye is trying to teach the narrator to move on to the next stage of awakening: of pure giving, based on the perfectly symmetrical thinking, as Manjŏk did.

혈서를 바치느라고 살을 물어 뗀 상처가 남아 있다. 이 행위는 만적이 깨달음으로 향하는 과정과 비교할 때, 두 번째 단계 정도에 해당한다. 그렇다면 원혜대사가 '나'의 바른손 식지를 들게 하여 말하려고 했던 것은 만적이 완벽한 대칭성의 사고에 바탕한 순수증여의 단계에 이르렀듯이, '나' 역시 더욱 큰 깨달음의 단계로 나아가라는 가르침의 뜻이라고 볼 수도 있을 것이다.

비평의 목소리

Critical Acclaim

김동리 문학, 그것은 물론 근대가 아니지만 근대 이전도 근대 이후도 아니었다. 근대의 초극도 물론 아니었다. 그것은 근대성의 논의 자체를 무화시키는 늪과 같은 것이었다. 어떠한 근대성 논의도 김동리 문학에 부딪히면 무(無)로 변해 버리는 것 같았다. 제로에 어떤 자연수를 곱해도 제로가 되듯 그것은 그러한 것처럼 내게 보이기 시작하였다.

김윤식, 『김동리와 그의 시대』, 민음사, 1995, 8쪽

김동리는 20세기 한국의 문학인들 중에서 전통 지향성의 계보를 대표하는 존재이다. 전통 지향성이란 주지하는

Kim Tong-ni's literature is neither modern—nor pre- or post-modern. Nor does it transcend modernity. It is like a dense landscape that nullifies a discussion of modernity. Any discussion of modernity turns into nothingness if it encounters Kim Tong-ni's literature. As zero becomes zero in mathematics no matter what natural number it is multiplied by, his literature nullifies the concept of modernity itself.

Kim Yun-shik, *Kim Tong-ni and his Times* (Seoul: Minumsa, 1995), 8

Among 20th-century Korean writers, Kim Tong-ni represents a tradition-oriented lineage, as op-

바와 같이 모더니티 지향성에 대립되는 개념이다. 그리고 20세기 내내 이 땅에서 모더니티 지향성이라는 말은 곧 서양 지향성과 대동소이한 뜻을 가지는 낱말로 인식되어 왔던 만큼, 모더니티 지향성에 대립되는 개념은 자연히 서양 지향성에도 대립되는 개념이 될 수밖에 없었다.

이동하, 「영웅 소설의 전통과 보수적 기독교의 문제」,

『김동리 전집⑤』, 민음사, 1995, 396쪽

김동리 문학의 가장 두드러진 특성은 어려운 상황 속에 있었지만 끝끝내 자신을 지켜내는 강한 주체가 그 세계의 중심에 우뚝 서 있다는 점이다. 그 강한 주체는 무당, 주모, 낙백한 전향자 등 하나같이 주변부 존재로서 중심부를 장악한 지배 질서 밖으로 밀려났으며 동시에 스스로 그 같은 소외를 선택한 외로운 존재이다. 말하자면 그는 '소외된/스스로를 소외시킨' 존재이다. 그는 또한 세계의 억압에 눌려 자신을 실현할 수 있는 가능성을 크게 제약당한 존재이다. 그럼에도 불구하고 그 강한 주체는 조금도 흔들리지 않으며 한 발짝도 물러나지 않는다.

정호웅, 『약전으로 읽는 문학사 1』, 소명출판, 2008, 466쪽

posed to a modernity-oriented one. And since an orientation toward modernity has been consistently understood as an orientation toward the West in Korea throughout the 20th century, opposition toward modernity meant opposition toward the West.

Lee Dong-ha, "The Tradition of the Hero Novel and the Problem of Conservative Christianity," *Collected Works of Kim Tong-ni* (Seoul: Minumsa, 1995), 396

The most salient characteristic of Kim Tong-ni's literature is a strong main character who defends himself in a trying situation and stands tall. These strong subjects are lonely, marginalized beings who have been pushed out of the mainstream that controls the center, as well as who have chosen alienation themselves. In other words, they are both alienated and alienating subjects. They are also beings whose possibility of realizing their potential is quite restricted by the oppression of the world. And yet these strong subjects never waver or retreat.

Jeong Ho-ung, *Literary History Read Through Abbreviated Biographies* (Seoul: Somyong, 2008), 466

김동리

김동리는 1913년 경북 경주에서 김임수의 5남매 중 3남으로 출생하였다. 아명은 창봉, 본명은 창위, 자는 시종이다. 경주제일교회부설학교인 계남소학교를 졸업하고 대구 계성중학과 서울 경신중학에서 수학하였다. 맏형 김범부의 영향 아래서 크게 성장할 수 있었는데, 김범부는 한국의 대표적 사상가 중 한 명이다. 1933년에 《조선일보》 신춘문예에 시 「백로」가 당선되고, 1935년과 1936년에는 각각 《조선중앙일보》와 《동아일보》의 신춘문예에 소설 「화랑의 후예」와 「산화(山火)」가 당선되었다. 1937년에는 다솔사에 속한 광명학원에서 교사로 활동하였고, 1938년 김월계와 혼인하였다. 1943년 사천의 양곡배급조합의 서기가 되었고, 1945년 사천청년회 회장이 되었다. 해방 이후 서울로 올라와 민족주의문학 진영의 선봉장격으로 활동하였으며, 전조선문필가협회에 참여하고 조연현 등과 청년문학가협회를 결성하여 초대 회장이 되었다. 김동석, 김병규 등의 사회주의 진영 문인들과 치열한 논쟁을 벌였으며, 이 기

Kim Tong-ni

Kim Tong-ni was born the third son among five children of Kim Im-su in Gyeongju in 1913. His childhood name was Ch'ang-bong, his official name is Ch'ang-wi, his nickname is Si-jong, and Tong-ni is his penname. After graduating from Kyenam Elementary School, affiliated with Kyŏngju Cheil Church, he studied at Kyesŏng Middle School in Daegu and Kyŏngsin Middle School in Seoul. His eldest brother, Kim Pŏm-bu, one of the most renowned thinkers in Korea at that time, had a strong influence on Kim Tong-ni. In 1933 Kim Tong-ni won the *Chosun Ilbo* Spring Literary Contest with his poem "A White Heron." In 1935 and 1936, he won the *Chosŏn Chung'ang Ilbo* Spring Literary Contest and the *Dong-A Ilbo* Spring Literary Contest, respectively, with his short stories "A Descendent of Hwarang" and "A Forest Fire." He taught at Kwangmyŏng Hagwŏn in 1937 and married Kim Wŏl-gye in 1938. He became a clerk at Sacheon Grain Distribution Association in 1943 and president of Sacheon Youth Association in 1945. After the liberation of Korea,

간에 경향신문사 문화부장, 민국일보사 편집부장, 전국 문화예술단체총연합회 선전부장, 《문예》의 주간, 서울 신문사 출판부 차장, 한국문학가협회 소설분과위원장 등을 역임하였다. 1953년 서라벌예술대학 문예창작학과 교수로 취임하였고, 1954년에 41세의 나이로 예술원 회원이 되었다. 1955년 아세아자유문학상, 1958년 대한민국예술원상, 1967년 3·1문화상, 1968년 국민훈장 동백장, 1970년 서울특별시문화상을 받았다. 1981년 대한민국예술원장이 되었고, 1982년에는 『을화』가 노벨 문학상 본선에 진출하였다. 뇌졸중으로 인한 오랜 투병 끝에 1995년 6월 17일 별세하였다. 창작집으로 『무녀도』(1947), 『황토기』(1949), 『귀환장정』(1951), 『사반의 십자가』(1958), 『등신불』(1963)과, 평론집으로 『문학과 인간』(1948), 『문학개론』(1952), 『문학이란 무엇인가』(1984) 등을 펴냈다.

he went to Seoul, where he spearheaded the nationalist literature camp, participating in the Nationwide Chosŏn Writers Association, establishing the Young Writers Association with Cho Yŏn-hyŏn and other writers, and serving as its president. He had fierce debates with socialist camp writers, like Kim Tong-sŏk and Kim Pyŏng-gyu. During this period, he worked as the chief editor of the culture page at *Kyunghyang Shinmun*; editor-in-chief of *Manguk Ilbo*; PR department chief of the Nationwide Culture and Arts Organization Association; editor-in-chief of the magazine *Munye*; vice director of the Publication Department of the *Seoul Shinmun*; and chair of the Fiction Committee at the Korean Writers Association. He became professor of creative writing at Sorabol College of Art in 1953, and a member of the National Academy of Arts in 1954 when he was forty-one. His honors and recognitions include the 1955 Asea Freedom Literature Award, the 1958 National Academy of Arts Award, the 1967 March 1st Culture Award, the 1968 Order of Civil Merit Camellia Medal, and the 1970 Seoul Culture Award. He became president of National Academy of Arts in 1981 and was nominated to Nobel Literature Laureates for his work *Ŭlhwa*. He died in 1995, after a long battle with a stroke. His publications include short-story collections, such as *Munyŏdo* [A portrait of a female shaman] (1947), *Hwangt'ogi* [A record of a barren land] (1949), and *Kwihwanjangjŏng* [A returned soldier] (1951), *Saban's Cross* (1958), *Tŭngsinbul* (1963), and the critical essay collections *Literature and Human Beings* (1948), *Introduction to Literature* (1952), and *What is Literature* (1984).

번역 **설순봉** Translated by Sŏl Sun-bong

1957년 서울대학교 영문학과를 졸업하고, 미국 뉴욕주립대학교에서 여성학을 공부했으며, 서울여자대학교, 성균관대학교 등에서 영문학을 가르쳤다. 김동리의 「사반의 십자가」, 이문열의 『황제를 위하여』를 비롯한 다수의 한국소설을 영어로 옮겼고, 헤밍웨이의 『무기여 잘 있거라』, 『노인과 바다』, 존 버거의 『그들의 노동에 함께 하였느니라』, 아이다 프루잇의 『중국의 딸』, 도리스 레싱의 『고양이는 정말 별나, 특히 루퍼스는…』, 토니 힐러만의 『고스트 웨이』 등을 한국어로 옮겼다.

Studied English Literature at Seoul National University and Miami University. Participated in the Women's Studies Program at State University of New York at Buffalo. Taught English Literature at SungKyunKwan University and Seoul Women's University. Translated English and American literary works into Korean including Ernest Hemingway's *For Whom the Bell Tolls*, and John Berger's *Into Their Labours*. Also translated Korean novels and stories including Yi Mun-yol's *Hail to the Emperor* and Park Wan-suh's *How I Kept Our House While My Husband was away*.

바이링궐 에디션 한국 대표 소설 107

등신불

2015년 1월 9일 초판 1쇄 발행

지은이 김동리 | **옮긴이** 설순봉 | **펴낸이** 김재범
기획위원 정은경, 전성태, 이경재 | **편집** 정수인, 이은혜, 김형욱, 윤단비 | **관리** 박신영
펴낸곳 (주)아시아 | **출판등록** 2006년 1월 27일 제406-2006-000004호
주소 서울특별시 동작구 서달로 161-1(흑석동 100-16)
전화 02.821.5055 | **팩스** 02.821.5057 | **홈페이지** www.bookasia.org
ISBN 979-11-5662-067-9 (set) | 979-11-5662-084-6 (04810)
값은 뒤표지에 있습니다.

Bi-lingual Edition Modern Korean Literature 107

Tŭngsin-bul

Written by Kim Tong-ni | **Translated by** Sŏl Sun-bong
Published by Asia Publishers | 161-1, Seodal-ro, Dongjak-gu, Seoul, Korea
Homepage Address www.bookasia.org | **Tel**. (822).821.5055 | **Fax**. (822).821.5057
First published in Korea by Asia Publishers 2015
ISBN 979-11-5662-067-9 (set) | 979-11-5662-084-6 (04810)

바이링궐 에디션 한국 대표 소설

한국문학의 가장 중요하고 첨예한 문제의식을 가진 작가들의 대표작을 주제별로 선정!
하버드 한국학 연구원 및 세계 각국의 한국문학 전문 번역진이 참여한 번역 시리즈!
미국 하버드대학교와 컬럼비아대학교 동아시아학과, 캐나다 브리티시컬럼비아대학교 아시아학과 등 해외 대학에서 교재로 채택!

바이링궐 에디션 한국 대표 소설 set 1

분단 Division

01 병신과 머저리-**이청준** The Wounded-**Yi Cheong-jun**
02 어둠의 혼-**김원일** Soul of Darkness-**Kim Won-il**
03 순이삼촌-**현기영** Sun-i Samch'on-**Hyun Ki-young**
04 엄마의 말뚝 1-**박완서** Mother's Stake I-**Park Wan-suh**
05 유형의 땅-**조정래** The Land of the Banished-**Jo Jung-rae**

산업화 Industrialization

06 무진기행-**김승옥** Record of a Journey to Mujin-**Kim Seung-ok**
07 삼포 가는 길-**황석영** The Road to Sampo-**Hwang Sok-yong**
08 아홉 켤레의 구두로 남은 사내-**윤흥길** The Man Who Was Left as Nine Pairs of Shoes-**Yun Heung-gil**
09 돌아온 우리의 친구-**신상웅** Our Friend's Homecoming-**Shin Sang-ung**
10 원미동 시인-**양귀자** The Poet of Wŏnmi-dong-**Yang Kwi-ja**

여성 Women

11 중국인 거리-**오정희** Chinatown-**Oh Jung-hee**
12 풍금이 있던 자리-**신경숙** The Place Where the Harmonium Was-**Shin Kyung-sook**
13 하나코는 없다-**최윤** The Last of Hanak'o-**Ch'oe Yun**
14 인간에 대한 예의-**공지영** Human Decency-**Gong Ji-young**
15 빈처-**은희경** Poor Man's Wife-**Eun Hee-kyung**

바이링궐 에디션 한국 대표 소설 set 2

자유 Liberty

16 필론의 돼지-**이문열** Pilon's Pig-**Yi Mun-yol**
17 슬로우 불릿-**이대환** Slow Bullet-**Lee Dae-hwan**
18 직선과 독가스-**임철우** Straight Lines and Poison Gas-**Lim Chul-woo**
19 깃발-**홍희담** The Flag-**Hong Hee-dam**
20 새벽 출정-**방현석** Off to Battle at Dawn-**Bang Hyeon-seok**

사랑과 연애 Love and Love Affairs

21 별을 사랑하는 마음으로-**윤후명** With the Love for the Stars-**Yun Hu-myong**
22 목련공원-**이승우** Magnolia Park-**Lee Seung-u**
23 칼에 찔린 자국-**김인숙** Stab-**Kim In-suk**
24 회복하는 인간-**한강** Convalescence-**Han Kang**
25 트렁크-**정이현** In the Trunk-**Jeong Yi-hyun**

남과 북 South and North

26 판문점-**이호철** Panmunjom-**Yi Ho-chol**
27 수난 이대-**하근찬** The Suffering of Two Generations-**Ha Geun-chan**
28 분지-**남정현** Land of Excrement-**Nam Jung-hyun**
29 봄 실상사-**정도상** Spring at Silsangsa Temple-**Jeong Do-sang**
30 은행나무 사랑-**김하기** Gingko Love-**Kim Ha-kee**

바이링궐 에디션 한국 대표 소설 set 3

서울 Seoul

31 눈사람 속의 검은 항아리-**김소진** The Dark Jar within the Snowman-**Kim So-jin**
32 오후, 가로지르다-**하성란** Traversing Afternoon-**Ha Seong-nan**
33 나는 봉천동에 산다-**조경란** I Live in Bongcheon-dong-**Jo Kyung-ran**
34 그렇습니까? 기린입니다-**박민규** Is That So? I'm A Giraffe-**Park Min-gyu**
35 성탄특선-**김애란** Christmas Specials-**Kim Ae-ran**

전통 Tradition

36 무자년의 가을 사흘-**서정인** Three Days of Autumn, 1948-**Su Jung-in**
37 유자소전-**이문구** A Brief Biography of Yuja-**Yi Mun-gu**
38 향기로운 우물 이야기-**박범신** The Fragrant Well-**Park Bum-shin**
39 월행-**송기원** A Journey under the Moonlight-**Song Ki-won**
40 협죽도 그늘 아래-**성석제** In the Shade of the Oleander-**Song Sok-ze**

아방가르드 Avant-garde

41 아겔다마-**박상륭** Akeldama-**Park Sang-ryoong**
42 내 영혼의 우물-**최인석** A Well in My Soul-**Choi In-seok**
43 당신에 대해서-**이인성** On You-**Yi In-seong**
44 회색 時-**배수아** Time In Gray-**Bae Su-ah**
45 브라운 부인-**정영문** Mrs. Brown-**Jung Young-moon**

바이링궐 에디션 한국 대표 소설 set 4

디아스포라 Diaspora

46 속옷-**김남일** Underwear-Kim Nam-il
47 상하이에 두고 온 사람들-**공선옥** People I Left in Shanghai-Gong Sun-ok
48 모두에게 복된 새해-**김연수** Happy New Year to Everyone-Kim Yeon-su
49 코끼리-**김재영** The Elephant-Kim Jae-young
50 먼지별-**이경** Dust Star-Lee Kyung

가족 Family

51 혜자의 눈꽃-**천승세** Hye-ja's Snow-Flowers-Chun Seung-sei
52 아베의 가족-**전상국** Ahbe's Family-Jeon Sang-guk
53 문 앞에서-**이동하** Outside the Door-Lee Dong-ha
54 그리고, 축제-**이혜경** And Then the Festival-Lee Hye-kyung
55 봄밤-**권여선** Spring Night-Kwon Yeo-sun

유머 Humor

56 오늘의 운세-**한창훈** Today's Fortune-Han Chang-hoon
57 새-**전성태** Bird-Jeon Sung-tae
58 밀수록 다시 가까워지는-**이기호** So Far, and Yet So Near-Lee Ki-ho
59 유리방패-**김중혁** The Glass Shield-Kim Jung-hyuk
60 전당포를 찾아서-**김종광** The Pawnshop Chase-Kim Chong-kwang

바이링궐 에디션 한국 대표 소설 set 5

관계 Relationship

61 도둑견습 – **김주영** Robbery Training-Kim Joo-young
62 사랑하라, 희망 없이 – **윤영수** Love, Hopelessly-Yun Young-su
63 봄날 오후, 과부 셋 – **정지아** Spring Afternoon, Three Widows-Jeong Ji-a
64 유턴 지점에 보물지도를 묻다 - **윤성희** Burying a Treasure Map at the U-turn-Yoon Sung-hee
65 쁘이거나 쯔이거나 - **백가흠** Puy, Thuy, Whatever-Paik Ga-huim

일상의 발견 Discovering Everyday Life

66 나는 음식이다 – **오수연** I Am Food-Oh Soo-yeon
67 트럭 – **강영숙** Truck-Kang Young-sook
68 통조림 공장 - **편혜영** The Canning Factory-Pyun Hye-young
69 꽃 – **부희령** Flowers-Pu Hee-ryoung
70 피의일요일 – **윤이형** BloodySunday-Yun I-hyeong

금기와 욕망 Taboo and Desire

71 북소리 - **송영** Drumbeat-**Song Yong**
72 발칸의 장미를 내게 주었네 - **정미경** He Gave Me Roses of the Balkans-**Jung Mi-kyung**
73 아무도 돌아오지 않는 밤 - **김숨** The Night Nobody Returns Home-**Kim Soom**
74 젓가락여자 - **천운영** Chopstick Woman-**Cheon Un-yeong**
75 아직 일어나지 않은 일 - **김미월** What Has Yet to Happen-**Kim Mi-wol**

바이링궐 에디션 한국 대표 소설 set 6

운명 Fate

76 언니를 놓치다 - **이경자** Losing a Sister-Lee Kyung-ja
77 아들 - **윤정모** Father and Son-Yoon Jung-mo
78 명두 - **구효서** Relics-Ku Hyo-seo
79 모독 - **조세희** Insult-Cho Se-hui
80 화요일의 강 - **손홍규** Tuesday River-Son Hong-gyu

미의 사제들 Aesthetic Priests

81 고수 - **이외수** Grand Master-Lee Oisoo
82 말을 찾아서 - **이순원** Looking for a Horse-Lee Soon-won
83 상춘곡 - **윤대녕** Song of Everlasting Spring-Youn Dae-nyeong
84 삭매와 자미 - **김별아** Sakmae and Jami-Kim Byeol-ah
85 저만치 혼자서 - **김훈** Alone Over There-Kim Hoon

식민지의 벌거벗은 자들 The Naked in the Colony

86 감자 - **김동인** Potatoes-Kim Tong-in
87 운수 좋은 날 - **현진건** A Lucky Day-Hyŏn Chin'gŏn
88 탈출기 - **최서해** Escape-Ch'oe So-hae
89 과도기 - **한설야** Transition-Han Seol-ya
90 지하촌 - **강경애** The Underground Village-Kang Kyŏng-ae